LIKE NOTHING ON EARTH

His hair stood up like a stiff brush and he commenced to run. Endless machines, all different, all making different things, plants, bugs, birds and fungoids. It was done by electroponics, atom fed to atom like brick after brick to build a house. It wasn't synthesis because that is assembly and this was assembly plus growth in response to unknown laws. In each and every one of these machines, he knew, was some key or code or cipher, some weird master-control of unimaginable complexity, which determined the precise pattern that each built. And the patterns were infinitely variable.

Here and there assemblies of apparatus stood silent, inactive, their tasks complete. Here and there other monstrous mounds of gadgetry were partly in pieces, either under repair or readied for modification. He stopped momentarily by a machine that had finished its job. It had fashioned a delicately shaded moth which now perched motionless, like a winged jewel, within its fabrication jar. The creature was perfect as far as he could tell. All it was waiting for was . . .

Beads of moisture popped out on his forehead. All that moth needed was the breath of life.

ERIC FRANK RUSSELL

LIKE NOTHING
ON EARTH

A Methuen Paperback

A Methuen Paperback

LIKE NOTHING ON EARTH

First published in Great Britain 1975
by Dobson Books Ltd
This edition published 1986
by Methuen London Ltd
11 New Fetter Lane, London EC4P 4EE

Copyright © 1975 Eric Frank Russell

Copyright © 'Allamagoosa' 1955 by Street & Smith Publications
Renewed 1983 by Davis Publications, Inc

Printed in Great Britain

British Library Cataloguing in Publication Data

Russell, Eric Frank
  Like nothing on earth.
  I. Title
  823′.912 [F]   PR6035.U66

  ISBN 0-413-60010-6

Acknowledgements
All stories from *Astounding Science Fiction*, published by
Street & Smith Publications, Inc, New York.

THE MECHANICAL MICE first appeared under the name of the late
Maurice G Hugi which was used as a pseudonym with his kind
permission.

CONTENTS

ALLAMAGOOSA

It was a long time since the *Bustler* had been so silent. She lay in the Sirian spaceport, her tubes cold, her shell particle-scarred, her air that of a long-distance runner exhausted at the end of a marathon. There was a good reason for this: she had returned from a lengthy trip by no means devoid of troubles.

Now, in port, well-deserved rest had been gained if only temporarily. Peace, sweet peace. No more bothers, no more crises, no more major upsets, no more dire predicaments such as crop up in free flight at least twice a day. Just peace.

Hah!

Captain McNaught reposed in his cabin, feet up on desk, and enjoyed the relaxation to the utmost. The engines were dead, their hellish pounding absent for the first time in months. Out there in the big city four hundred of his crew were making whoopee under a brilliant sun. This evening, when First Officer Gregory returned to take charge, he was going to go into the fragrant twilight and make the rounds of neon-lit civilization.

That was the beauty of making landfall at long last. Men could give way to themselves, blow off surplus steam, each according to his fashion. No duties, no worries, no dangers, no responsibilities in spaceport. A haven of safety and comfort for tired rovers.

Again, hah!

Burman, the chief radio officer, entered the cabin. He was one of the half-dozen remaining on duty and bore the expression of a man who can think of twenty better things to do.

'Relayed signal just come in, sir.' Handing the paper across he waited for the other to look at it and perhaps dictate a reply.

Taking the sheet, McNaught removed the feet from his desk, sat erect and read the message aloud.

Terran Headquarters to Bustler. *Remain Siriport pending further orders. Rear Admiral Vane W. Cassidy due there seventeenth. Feldman. Navy Op. Command, Sirisec.*

He looked up, all happiness gone from his leathery features, and groaned.

'Something wrong?' asked Burman, vaguely alarmed.

McNaught pointed at three thin books on his desk. 'The middle one. Page twenty.'

Leafing through it, Burman found an item that said: *Vane W. Cassidy, R-Ad. Head Inspector Ships and Stores.*

Burman swallowed hard. 'Does that mean – ?'

'Yes, it does,' said McNaught without pleasure. 'Back to training-college and all its rigmarole. Paint and soap, spit and polish.' He put on an officious expression, adopted a voice to match it. 'Captain, you have only seven ninety-nine emergency rations. Your allocation is eight hundred. Nothing in your logbook accounts for the missing one. Where is it? What happened to it? How is it that one of the men's kit lacks an officially issued pair of suspenders? Did you report his loss?'

'Why does he pick on us?' asked Burman, appalled. 'He's never chivvied us before.'

'That's why,' informed McNaught, scowling at the wall. 'It's our turn to be stretched across the barrel.' His gaze found the calendar. 'We have three days – and we'll need 'em! Tell Second Officer Pike to come here at once.'

Burman departed gloomily. In short time Pike entered. His face reaffirmed the old adage that bad news travels fast.

'Make out an indent,' ordered McNaught, 'for one hundred gallons of plastic paint, Navy-gray, approved quality. Make out another for thirty gallons of interior white enamel. Take them to spaceport stores right away. Tell them to deliver by six this evening along with our correct issue of brushes and sprayers. Grab up any cleaning material that's going for free.'

'The men won't like this,' remarked Pike, feebly.

'They're going to love it,' McNaught asserted. 'A bright and shiny ship, all spic and span, is good for morale. It says so in that book. Get moving and put those indents in. When you come back, find the stores and equipment sheets and bring them here. We've got to check stocks before Cassidy arrives. Once he's here we'll have no chance to make up shortages or smuggle out any extra items we happened to find in our hands.'

'Very well, sir.' Pike went out wearing the same expression as Burman's.

Lying back in his chair McNaught muttered to himself. There was a feeling in his bones that something was sure to cause a last-minute ruckus. A shortage of any item would be serious enough unless covered by a previous report. A surplus would be bad, very bad. The former implied carelessness or misfortune. The latter suggested barefaced theft of government property in circumstances condoned by the commander.

For instance, there was that recent case of Williams of the heavy cruiser *Swift*. He'd heard of it over the spacevine when out around Bootes. Williams had been found in unwitting command of eleven reels of electric fence wire when his official issue was ten. It had taken a court-martial to decide that the extra reel – which had formidable barter-value on a certain planet – had not been stolen from space-stores, or, in sailor jargon, 'teleportated aboard.' But Williams had been reprimanded. And that did not help promotion.

He was still rumbling discontentedly when Pike returned bearing a folder of foolscap sheets.

'Going to start right away, sir?'

'We'll have to.' He heaved himself erect, mentally bidded goodbye to time off and a taste of the bright lights. 'It'll take long enough to work right through from bow to tail. I'll leave the men's kit inspection to the last.'

Marching out of the cabin, he set forth toward the bow, Pike following with broody reluctance.

As they passed the open main lock Peaslake observed them, bounded eagerly up the gangway and joined behind. A pukka member of the crew, he was a large dog whose ancestors had been more enthusiastic than selective. He wore with pride a big collar inscribed: *Peaslake – Property of S. S. Bustler.* His chief duties, ably performed, were to keep alien rodents off the ship and, on rare occasions, smell out dangers not visible to human eyes.

The three paraded forward, McNaught and Pike in the manner of men grimly sacrificing pleasure for the sake of duty, Peaslake with the panting willingness of one ready for any new game no matter what.

Reaching the bow-cabin, McNaught dumped himself in the pilot's seat, took the folder from the other. 'You know this stuff better than me – the chart room is where I shine. So I'll read them out while you look them over.' He opened the folder, started on the first page. 'K1 Beam compass, type D, one of.'

'Check,' said Pike.

'K2. Distance and direction indicator, electronic, type JJ, one of.'

'Check.'

'K3. Port and starboard gravitic meters, Casini models, one pair.'

'Check.'

Peaslake planted his head in McNaught's lap, blinked soulfully and whined. He was beginning to get the others' viewpoint. This tedious itemizing and checking was a hell of a game. McNaught consolingly lowered a hand and played with Peaslake's ears while he ploughed his way down the list.

'K187. Foam rubber cushions, pilot and co-pilot, one pair.'

'Check.'

By the time First Officer Gregory appeared they had reached the tiny intercom cubby and poked around it in semidarkness. Peaslake had long departed in disgust.

'M24. Spare minispeakers, three inch, type T2, one set of six.'

'Check.'

Looking in, Gregory popped his eyes and said, 'What's going on?'

'Major inspection due soon.' McNaught glanced at his watch. 'Go see if stores has delivered a load and if not why not. Then you'd better give me a hand and let Pike take a few hours off.'

'Does this mean land-leave is cancelled?'

'You bet it does – until after Hizonner has been and gone.' He glanced at Pike. 'When you get into the city search around and send back any of the crew you can find. No arguments or excuses. Also no alibis and/or delays. It's an order.'

Pike registered unhappiness. Gregory glowered at him, went away, came back and said, 'Stores will have the stuff here in twenty minutes' time.' With bad grace he watched Pike depart.

'M47. Intercom cable, woven-wire protected, three drums.'

'Check,' said Gregory, mentally kicking himself for returning at the wrong time.

The task continued until late in the evening, was resumed early next morning. By that time three-quarters of the men were hard at work inside and outside the vessel, doing their jobs as though sentenced to them for crimes contemplated but not yet committed.

Moving around the ship's corridors and catwalks had to be done crab-fashion, with a nervous sidewise edging. Once again it was being demonstrated that the Terran life form suffers from ye fear of wette paynt. The first smearer would have ten years willed off his unfortunate life.

It was in these conditions, in midafternoon of the second day, that McNaught's bones proved their feelings had been prophetic. He recited the ninth page while Jean Blanchard confirmed the presence and actual existence of all items enumerated. Two-thirds of the way down they hit the rocks, metaphorically speaking, and commenced to sink fast.

McNaught said boredly, 'V1097. Drinking bowl, enamel, one of.'

'Is zis,' said Blanchard, tapping it.

'V1098. Offog, one.'

'*Quoi?*' asked Blanchard, staring.

'V1098. Offog, one,' repeated McNaught. 'Well, why are you looking thunderstruck? This is the ship's galley. You're the head cook. You know what's supposed to be in the galley, don't you? Where's this offog?'

'Never hear of heem,' stated Blanchard, flatly.

'You must have. It's on this equipment-sheet in plain, clear type. Offog, one, it says. It was here when we were fitted out four years ago. We checked it ourselves and signed for it.'

'I signed for nossings called offog,' Blanchard denied. 'In the cuisine zere is no such sing.'

'Look!' McNaught scowled and showed him the sheet.

Blanchard looked and sniffed disdainfully. 'I have here zee electronic oven, one of. I have jacketed boilers, gradu-ated capacities, one set. I have bain marie pans, seex of. But no offog. Never heard of heem. I do not know of heem.' He spread his hands and shrugged. 'No offog.'

'There's got to be,' McNaught insisted. 'What's more, when Cassidy arrives there'll be hell to pay if there isn't.'

'You find heem,' Blanchard suggested.

'You got a certificate from the International Hotels School of Cookery. You got a certificate from the Cordon Bleu College of Cuisine. You got a certificate with three credits from the Space-Navy Feeding Center,' McNaught pointed out. 'All that – and you don't know what an offog is.'

'*Nom d'un chien!*' ejaculated Blanchard, waving his arms around. 'I tell you ten t'ousand time zere is no offog. Zere never was an offog. Escoffier heemself could not find zee offog of vich zere is none. Am I a magician perhaps?'

'It's part of the culinary equipment,' McNaught main-tained. 'It must be because it's on page nine. And page nine means its proper home is in the galley, care of the head cook.'

'Like hail it does,' Blanchard retorted. He pointed at a metal box on the wall. 'Intercom booster. Is zat mine?'

McNaught thought it over, conceded, 'No, it's Burman's. His stuff rambles all over the ship.'

'Zen ask heem for zis bloody offog,' said Blanchard, triumphantly.

'I will. If it's not yours it must be his. Let's finish this checking first. If I'm not systematic and thorough Cassidy will jerk off my insignia.' His eyes sought the list. 'V1099. Inscribed collar, leather, brass studded, dog, for the use of. No need to look for that. I saw it myself five minutes ago.' He ticked the item, continued, 'V1100. Sleeping basket, woven reed, one of.'

'Is zis,' said Blanchard, kicking it into a corner.

'V1101. Cushion, foam rubber, to fit sleeping basket, one of.'

'Half of,' Blanchard contradicted. 'In four years he has chewed away other half.'

'Maybe Cassidy will let us indent for a new one. It doesn't matter. We're okay so long as we can produce the half we've got.' McNaught stood up, closed the folder. 'That's the lot for here. I'll go see Burman about this missing item.'

The inventory party moved on.

Burman switched off a UHF receiver, removed his earplugs and raised a questioning eyebrow.

'In the galley we're short an offog,' explained McNaught. 'Where is it?'

'Why ask me? The galley is Blanchard's bailiwick.'

'Not entirely. A lot of your cables run through it. You've two terminal boxes in there, also an automatic switch and an intercom booster. Where's the offog?'

'Never heard of it,' said Burman, baffled.

McNaught shouted, 'Don't tell me that! I'm already fed up hearing Blanchard saying it. Four years back we had an offog. It says so here. This is our copy of what we checked and signed for. It says we signed for an offog. Therefore we must have one. It's got to be found before Cassidy gets here.'

'Sorry, sir,' sympathized Burman. 'I can't help you.'

'You can think again,' advised McNaught. 'Up in the bow there's a direction and distance indicator. What do *you* call it?'

'A didin,' said Burman, mystified.

'And,' McNaught went on, pointing at the pulse transmitter, 'what do you call *that*?'

'The opper-popper.'

'Baby names, see? Didin and opper-popper. Now rack your brains and remember what you called an offog four years ago.'

'Nothing,' asserted Burman, 'has ever been called an offog to my knowledge.'

'Then,' demanded McNaught, 'why did we sign for one?'

'I didn't sign for anything. You did all the signing.'

'While you and others did the checking. Four years ago, presumably in the galley, I said, "Offog, one," and either you or Blanchard pointed to it and said, "Check." I took somebody's word for it. I have to take other specialists' words for it. I am an expert navigator, familiar with all the latest navigational gadgets but not with other stuff. So I'm compelled to rely on people who know what an offog is – or ought to.'

Burman had a bright thought. 'All kinds of oddments were dumped in the main lock, the corridors and the galley when we were fitted-out. We had to sort through a deal of stuff and stash it where it properly belonged, remember? This offog-thing might be any place today. It isn't necessarily my responsibility or Blanchard's.'

'I'll see what the other officers say,' agreed McNaught, conceding the point. 'Gregory, Worth, Sanderson or one of the others may be coddling the item. Wherever it is, it's got to be found. Or accounted for in full if it's been expended.'

He went out. Burman pulled a face, inserted his earplugs, resumed fiddling with his apparatus. An hour later McNaught came back wearing a scowl.

'Positively,' he announced with ire, 'there is no such thing on the ship. Nobody knows of it. Nobody can so much as guess at it.'

'Cross it off and report it lost,' Burman suggested.

'What, when we're hard aground? You know as well as I do that loss and damage must be signaled at the time of occurrence. If I tell Cassidy the offog went west in space, he'll want to know when, where, how and why it wasn't signalled. There'll be a real ruckus if the contraption happens to be valued at half a million credits. I can't dismiss it with an airy wave of the hand.'

'What's the answer then?' inquired Burman, innocently ambling straight into the trap.

'There's one and only one,' McNaught announced. '*You* will manufacture an offog.'

'Who? Me?' said Burman, twitching his scalp.

'You and no other. I'm fairly sure the thing is your pigeon, anyway.'

'Why?'

'Because it's typical of the baby names used for your kind of stuff. I'll bet a month's pay that an offog is some sort of scientific allamagoosa. Something to do with fog, perhaps. Maybe a blind-approach gadget.'

'The blind-approach transceiver is called "the fumbly,"' Burman informed.

'There you are!' said McNaught as if that clinched it. 'So you will make an offog. It will be completed by six tomorrow evening and ready for my inspection then. It had better be convincing, in fact pleasing. In fact its function will be convincing.'

Burman stood up, let his hands dangle, and said in hoarse tones, 'How can I make an offog when I don't even know what it is?'

'Neither does Cassidy know,' McNaught pointed out, leering at him. 'He's more of a quantity surveyor than anything else. As such he counts things, looks at things, certifies that they exist, accepts advice on whether they are functionally satisfactory or worn out. All we need do is concoct an imposing allamagoosa and tell him it's the offog.'

'Holy Moses!' said Burman, fervently.

'Let us not rely on the dubious assistance of Biblical characters,' McNaught reproved. 'Let us use the brains that God has given us. Get a grip on your soldering-iron and make a topnotch offog by six tomorrow evening. That's an order!'

He departed, satisfied with this solution. Behind him,

Burman gloomed at the wall and licked his lips once, twice.

Rear Admiral Vane W. Cassidy arrived right on time. He was a short, paunchy character with a florid complexion and eyes like those of a long-dead fish. His gait was an important strut.

'Ah, captain, I trust that you have everything shipshape.'

'Everything usually is,' assured McNaught, glibly. 'I see to that.' He spoke with conviction.

'Good!' approved Cassidy. 'I like a commander who takes his responsibilities seriously. Much as I regret saying so, there are a few who do not.' He marched through the main lock, his cod-eyes taking note of the fresh white enamel. 'Where do you prefer to start, bow or tail?'

'My equipment-sheets run from bow backward. We may as well deal with them the way they're set.'

'Very well.' He trotted officiously toward the nose, paused on the way to pat Peaslake and examine his collar. 'Well cared-for, I see. Has the animal proved useful?'

'He saved five lives on Mardia by barking a warning.'

'The details have been entered in your log, I suppose?'

'Yes, sir. The log is in the chart room awaiting your inspection.'

'We'll get to it in due time.' Reaching the bow-cabin, Cassidy took a seat, accepted the folder from McNaught, started off at businesslike pace. 'K1. Beam compass, type D, one of.'

'This is it, sir,' said McNaught, showing him.

'Still working properly?'

'Yes, sir.'

They carried on, reached the intercom cubby, the computer room, a succession of other places back to the galley. Here, Blanchard posed in freshly laundered white clothes and eyed the newcomer warily.

'V147. Electronic oven, one of.'

'Is zis,' said Blanchard, pointing with disdain.

'Satisfactory?' inquired Cassidy, giving him the fishy-eye.

'Not beeg enough,' declared Blanchard. He encompassed the entire galley with an expressive gesture. 'Nossings beeg enough. Place too small. Eversings too small. I am chef de cuisine an' she is a cuisine like an attic.'

'This is a warship, not a luxury liner,' Cassidy snapped. He frowned at the equipment-sheet. 'V148. Timing device, electronic oven, attachment thereto, one of.'

'Is zis,' spat Blanchard, ready to sling it through the nearest port if Cassidy would first donate the two pins.

Working his way down the sheet, Cassidy got nearer and nearer while nervous tension built up. Then he reached the critical point and said, 'V1098. Offog, one.'

'*Morbleu*!' said Blanchard, shooting sparks from his eyes, 'I have say before an' I say again, zere never was – '

'The offog is in the radio room, sir,' McNaught chipped in hurriedly.

'Indeed?' Cassidy took another look at the sheet. 'Then why is it recorded along with galley equipment?'

'It was placed in the galley at time of fitting-out. sir. It's one of those portable instruments left to us to fix up where most suitable.'

'Hm-m-m! Then it should have been transferred to the radio room list. Why didn't you transfer it?'

'I thought it better to wait for your authority to do so, sir.'

The fish-eyes registered gratification. 'Yes, that is quite proper of you, captain. I will transfer it now.' He crossed the item from sheet nine, initialed it, entered it on sheet sixteen, initialed that. 'V1099. Inscribed collar, leather . . . oh, yes, I've seen that. The dog was wearing it.'

He ticked it. An hour later he strutted into the radio room. Burman stood up, squared his shoulders but could not keep his feet or hands from fidgeting. His eyes protruded slightly and kept straying toward McNaught in silent appeal. He was like a man wearing a porcupine in his britches.

'V1098. Offog, one,' said Cassidy in his usual tone of brooking no nonsense.

Moving with the jerkiness of a slightly uncoordinated robot, Burman pawed a small box fronted with dials, switches and coloured lights. It looked like a radio ham's idea of a fruit machine. He knocked down a couple of switches. The lights came on, played around in intriguing combinations.

'This is it, sir,' he informed with difficulty.

'Ah!' Cassidy left his chair and moved across for a closer look. 'I don't recall having seen this item before. But there are so many different models of the same things. Is it still operating efficiently?'

'Yes, sir.'

'It's one of the most useful things in the ship,' contributed McNaught, for good measure.

'What does it *do*?' inquired Cassidy, inviting Burman to cast a pearl of wisdom before him.

Burman paled.

Hastily, McNaught said, 'A full explanation would be rather involved and technical but, to put it as simply as possible, it enables us to strike a balance between opposing gravitational fields. Variations in lights indicate the extent and degree of unbalance at any given time.'

'It's a clever idea,' added Burman, made suddenly reckless by this news, 'based upon Finagle's Constant.'

'I see,' said Cassidy, not seeing at all. He resumed his seat, ticked the offog and carried on. 'Z44. Switchboard, automatic, forty-line intercom, one of.'

'Here it is, sir.'

Cassidy glanced at it, returned his gaze to the sheet. The others used his momentary distraction to mop perspiration from their foreheads.

Victory had been gained.

All was well.

For the third time, hah!

Rear Admiral Vane W. Cassidy departed pleased and complimentary. Within one hour the crew bolted to town. McNaught took turns with Gregory at enjoying the gay lights. For the next five days all was peace and pleasure.

On the sixth day Burman brought in a signal, dumped it upon McNaught's desk and waited for the reaction. He had an air of gratification, the pleasure of one whose virtue is about to be rewarded.

Terran Headquarters to Bustler. *Return here immediately for overhaul and refitting. Improved power plant to be installed. Feldman. Navy Op. Command. Sirisec.*

'Back to Terra,' commented McNaught, happily. 'And an overhaul will mean at least one month's leave.' He eyed Burman. 'Tell all officers on duty to go to town at once and order the crew aboard. The men will come running when they know why.'

'Yes, sir,' said Burman, grinning.

Everyone was still grinning two weeks later when the Siriport had receded far behind and Sol had grown to a vague speck in the sparkling mist of the bow starfield. Eleven weeks still to go, but it was worth it. Back to Terra. Hurrah!

In the captain's cabin the grins abruptly vanished one evening when Burman suddenly developed the willies. He marched in, chewed his bottom lip while waiting for McNaught to finish writing in the log.

Finally, McNaught pushed the book away, glanced up, frowned. 'What's the matter with you? Got a bellyache or something?'

'No, sir. I've been thinking.'

'Does it hurt that much?'

'I've been thinking,' persisted Burman in funereal tones. 'We're going back for overhaul. You know what that means? We'll walk off the ship and a horde of experts will walk onto it.' He stared tragically at the other. 'Experts, I said.'

'Naturally they'll be experts,' McNaught agreed. 'Equipment cannot be tested and brought up to scratch by a bunch of dopes.'

'It will require more than a mere expert to bring the offog up to scratch,' Burman pointed out. 'It'll need a genius.'

McNaught rocked back, swapped expressions like changing masks. 'Jumping Judas! I'd forgotten all about that thing. When we get to Terra we won't blind *those* boys with science.'

'No, sir, we won't,' endorsed Burman. He did not add 'any more' but his face shouted aloud, 'You got me into this. You get me out of it.' He waited a time while McNaught did some intense thinking, then prompted, 'What do you suggest, sir?'

Slowly the satisfied smile returned to McNaught's features as he answered, 'Break up the contraption and feed it into the disintegrator.'

'That doesn't solve the problem,' said Burman. 'We'll still be short an offog.'

'No we won't. Because I'm going to signal its loss owing to the hazards of space-service.' He closed one eye in an emphatic wink. 'We're in free flight right now.' He reached for a message-pad and scribbled on it while Burman stood by vastly relieved.

Bustler to *Terran Headquarters. Item V1098, Offog one, came apart under gravitational stress while passing through twin-sun field Hector Major-Minor. Material used as fuel. McNaught, Commander.* Bustler.

Burman took it to the radio room and beamed it Earthward. All was peace and progress for another two days. The next time he went to the captain's cabin he went running and worried.

'General call, sir,' he announced breathlessly and thrust the message into the other's hands.

Terran Headquarters for relay all sectors. Urgent and Important. All ships grounded forthwith. Vessels in flight under official orders will make for nearest spaceport pending further instructions. Welling. Alarm and Rescue Command. Terra.

'Something's gone bust,' commented McNaught, undisturbed. He traipsed to the chart room, Burman following. Consulting the charts, he dialed the intercom phone, got Pike in the bow and ordered, 'There's a panic. All ships grounded. We've got to make for Zaxtedport, about three days' run away. Change course at once. Starboard seventeen degrees, declination ten.' Then he cut off, griped, 'Bang goes that sweet month on Terra. I never did like Zaxted, either. It stinks. The crew will feel murderous about this and I don't blame them.'

'What d'you think has happened, sir?' asked Burman. He looked both uneasy and annoyed.

'Heaven alone knows. The last general call was seven years ago when the *Starider* exploded halfway along the Mars run. They grounded every ship in existence while they investigated the cause.' He rubbed his chin, pondered, went on, 'And the call before that one was when the entire crew of the *Blowgun* went nuts. Whatever it is this time, you can bet it's serious.'

'It wouldn't be the start of a space war?'

'Against whom?' McNaught made a gesture of contempt. 'Nobody has the ships with which to oppose us. No, it's something technical. We'll learn of it eventually. They'll tell us before we reach Zaxted or soon afterward.'

They did tell him. Within six hours. Burman rushed in with face full of horror.

'What's eating you now?' demanded McNaught, staring at him.

'The offog,' stuttered Burman. He made motions as though brushing off invisible spiders.

'What of it?'

'It's a typographical error. In your copy it should read off. dog.'

The commander stared owlishly.

'Off. dog?' echoed McNaught, making it sound like foul language.

'See for yourself.' Dumping the signal on the desk, Burman bolted out, left the door swinging. McNaught scowled after him, picked up the message.

Terran Headquarters to Bustler. *Your report V1098, ship's official dog Peaslake. Detail fully circumstances and manner in which animal came apart under gravitational stress. Cross-examine crew and signal all coincidental symptoms experienced by them. Urgent and Important. Welling. Alarm and Rescue Command. Terra.*

In the privacy of his cabin McNaught commenced to eat his nails. Every now and again he went a little cross-eyed as he examined them for nearness to the flesh.

HOBBYIST

The ship arced out of a golden sky and landed with a whoop and a wallop that cut down a mile of lush vegetation. Another half-mile of alien growths turned black and drooped to ashes under the final flicker of the tail rocket blasts. That arrival was spectacular, full of verve and worthy of several columns in any Earthly newspaper. But the nearest journal was distant by a goodly slice of a lifetime and there was no waiting human being to record what this far corner of the cosmos viewed as the pettiest of events. So the ship squatted tired and still at the foremost end of its ashy blast-track and the sky glowed down and the green world brooded solemnly all around.

Within the transpex control dome Steve Ander sat and thought things over. It was his habit to think things over very carefully. Astronauts were not the impulsive dare-devils so dear to the stereopticon-loving public. They couldn't afford to be. The hazards of the profession demanded an infinite capacity for cautious, contemplative thought. Five minutes of careful consideration had pre-vented many a collapsed lung, many a leaky heart, many a fractured frame. Steve valued his skeleton. He wasn't conceited about it and he had no reason to believe it in any way superior to anyone else's skeleton. But he'd had it a long time, found it quite satisfactory, couldn't imagine himself without it and had an intense desire to keep it – intact.

Therefore, while the tail tubes cooled off with their usual creaking contractions, he squatted in the control seat, stared through the dome with eyes made unseeing by deep preoccupation, and performed a few thinks.

Firstly, he'd made a rough estimate of this world during his hectic approach. As nearly as he could judge it was about ten times the size of Terra. Yet his weight didn't seem to be formidable. Of course, one's notions of weight tended to be somewhat wild when for many weeks one's own heaviness has shot far up or far down in between periods of weightlessness. The most reasonable estimate had to be based on muscular reaction. If you felt as sluggish as a Saturnian sloth, your weight was way up. If you felt as powerful as Angus McKittrick's bull, it was down.

Normal weight meant Terrestrial mass despite this planet's tenfold volume. That meant light plasma. And that meant lack of heavy elements. No thorium. No nickel. No nickel-thorium alloy. Ergo, no getting back. The Kingston-Kane atomic motors required fuel in the form of ten gauge nickel-thorium alloy wire fed directly in the vaporizers. Denatured plutonium would do but it didn't occur in natural form and had to be made. He had forty-five and a half inches of nickel-thorium left on the feed-spool. Not enough. He was here for keeps.

A wonderful thing, logic. You could start from the simple premise that when you were seated your backside was no flatter than usual and work your way to the inevitable conclusion that you were a space-roamer no more. You'd become a local native. Destiny had you tagged as suitable for the status of oldest inhabitant.

Steve pulled a face and said, 'Darn!' Given the circumstances, it was a feeble comment, but he felt it profitless to seek words more adequate.

As for his face, it didn't have to be pulled far. Nature

had given it a good start. That is to say, it wasn't handsome. It was a long, lean, nut-brown face with pronounced jaw-muscles, prominent cheekbones and a thin, hooked nose. This, with his dark eyes and black hair, gave him a hawklike appearance. Friends talked to him about tepees and tomahawks when they wanted him to feel at home.

Well, he wasn't going to feel at home any more; not unless this other-world jungle held intelligent life dopey enough to swap a hundred yards of ten gauge nickel-thorium wire for a pair of old boots. Or unless some dopey search-party from Earth was clever enough to pick this cosmic dust-mote out of a cloud of motes and took him back home. He estimated this as one chance out of uncountable millions, a chance so unlikely as to verge upon the impossible.

Reaching for his everflo stylus and the ship's logbook, he opened the log, surveyed its most recent entries.

'Eighteenth day: the spatial convulsion has now flung me past rotal-range of Rigel. Am being swept into uncharted regions.'

'Twenty-fourth day: arm of convulsion now tails back seven parsecs. Robot recorder out of gear. Angle of throw unchanged nine times today.'

'Twenty-ninth day: now beyond arm of the convulsive swirl and regaining control. Velocity far beyond range of the astrometer. Applying braking rockets cautiously. Fuel reserve: fourteen hundred yards.'

'Thirty-seventh day: making for planetary system now within reach.'

He frowned, his jaw-muscles lumped and he wrote slowly and legibly, 'Forty-first day: landed on planet unknown, primary unknown, galactic area standard reference and sector numbers unknown. No cosmic formations were identifiable when observed shortly before landing. Angles of offshoot and speed of transit not recorded and impossible to estimate. Condition of ship: workable. Fuel reserve: forty-five and one-half inches.'

Closing the log, he frowned again, rammed the stylus into its desk-grip and muttered, 'Now to check on the outside air and see how the best girl's doing.'

The Radson register had three simple dials. The first recorded outside pressure at thirteen point seven pounds, a reading he noted with some satisfaction. The second said that oxygen content was high. The third had a bi-coloured dial, half white, half red, and its needle stood in the middle of the white.

'Breathable,' he grunted, clipping down the register's lid. Crossing the tiny control-room, he slid aside a metal panel, looking into the padded compartment behind.

'Coming out, Beauteous?' he asked.

'Steve loves Laura?' demanded a plaintive voice.

'You bet he does!' he responded with becoming passion. He shoved an arm into the compartment and brought out a large, gaudily coloured macaw. 'Does Laura love Steve?'

'I'm not for sale!' shouted Laura. 'I'm not for sale!' Climbing up his arm and with the help of its beak, the bird perched on his shoulder. He could feel its weight and the grip of its powerful claws. It regarded him with a beady and brilliant eye, then rubbed its crimson head against his left ear. 'Time flies,' it said and let go a harsh cackle.

'Don't mention it,' he reproved. 'Right now there's plenty to remind me of the fact without you emphasizing it.'

Reaching up, he scratched her poll while she stretched and bowed with absurd delight. He was fond of Laura. She was far more than a mere pet. She was a *bona fide* member of the crew, issued with her own rations and drawing her own pay. Every probe ship had a crew of two: one man, one macaw. When first he'd heard of it the practice had seemed crazy – but when he found the reasons they made sense.

'Lonely men probing far beyond the edge of the charts

get queer psychological troubles if left to run loose without some kind of link with Mother Earth. A macaw provides the necessary companionship – and more. It's the space-hardiest creature we've got, its weight is negligible, it can talk and amuse and it can fend for itself to a surprising extent. On land it will often sense dangers before you do. Any strange fruit or grain it may eat will be safe for you to eat. Many a man's life has been saved by his macaw. Take care of yours, my boy, and it will take care of you.'

Yes, they'd look after each other, Terrestrials both. It was almost a symbiosis of the spaceways. Before the era of lengthy astro-navigation nobody had thought of such an arrangement, though similar things had been done before. Miners and their canaries, for example.

Moving over to the small airlock, he did not bother to operate the pump. It wasn't necessary with so small a difference between internal and external pressures. Opening both doors, he let a little of his more compacted air sigh out, stood on the rim of the lock, jumped out. Laura fluttered from his shoulder as he leaped, followed him with a flurry of wings, got her talons into the shoulder of his jacket as he staggered upright.

The pair went around the ship, silently surveying its condition. Front braking nozzles okay, rear steering flares okay, tail propulsion tubes okay. All were badly scored but still usable. The skin of the vessel was likewise scored but intact. Theoretically, three to four months' supply of food and maybe a thousand yards of wire could get her home. But only theoretically. Steve had no illusions about the matter. The odds were heavily against him even if given the means to move. How do you navigate from you-don't-know-where to you-don't-know-where-else? Answer: you stroke a rabbit's foot and hope for the best. Without hope there is nothing, nothing what . . . so . . . ever.

'Well,' he said, rounding the tail, 'it's something in which to live. It'll save us the bother of building a shanty. Way back on Terra we'd be asked a diabolical price for an all-metal streamlined bungalow, so I guess we're mighty lucky. I'll make a garden here, and a rockery there, and build a swimming pool out back. You can wear a pretty frock and do all the cooking.'

'Who, me?' yelled Laura, incredulously. 'Yawk!'

Turning, he had a look at the nearest vegetation. It was of all heights, shapes and sizes, of all shades of green with a few tending towards blueness. There was something peculiar about these growths but he was unable to decide exactly where their strangeness lay. It wasn't that they were alien and unfamiliar – one expected that on every new world – it was an underlying oddness that they had in common. They had a vague, shadowy air of being not quite right in some basic respect impossible to define.

A small plant was growing right at his feet. It was a foot high, green in colour and monocotyledonous. Looked at as a thing in itself, there was nothing wrong with it. Near to it flourished a bush of darker hue, a yard high, with green firlike needles in lieu of leaves, and pale, waxy berries scattered all over it. That, too, was innocent enough when studied apart from its neighbours. Beside it grew a similar plant differing only in that its needles were longer and its berries a bright pink. Beyond these towered a cactus-like object dragged out of somebody's drunken dreams, and beside it stood an umbrella-frame which had taken root and produced little purple pods. Individually, they were acceptable. Collectively, they made the discerning mind search uneasily for it knew not what.

That eerie feature had Steve stumped. Whatever it was, he couldn't nail it down. Definitely there was something present far stranger than the mere strangeness of new forms of plant life. He dismissed the problem with a shrug. Time enough to trouble about such matters after he had dealt with others more urgent such as, for example, the location and purity of the nearest water supply.

A mile away lay a lake of some liquid that might be water. He'd seen it glittering in the sunlight as he'd made his descent, and he had tried to land fairly near to it. If it wasn't drinkable water, well, that would be his tough luck and he'd have to search someplace else. At worst, the tiny fuel reserve would be enough to permit one circumnavigation of the planet before the ship became pinned down for ever. Water he must have if he wasn't going to end up imitating the mummy of Rameses the Second.

Reaching high, he grasped the rim of the airlock, dextrously muscled himself upward and through it. For a couple of minutes he moved around inside the ship, then reappeared with a four-gallon freezocan which he tossed to the ground. Then he dug out his popgun, a belt of explosive shells, and let down the folding ladder from lock to surface. He'd need that ladder. He could do a gymnastic trick to get himself through a hole seven feet above ground but not with fifty pounds of can and water.

Finally he locked both the inner and outer airlock doors, skipped down the ladder, picked up the can. From the way he'd made his landing the lake should be directly bow-on relative to the vessel and somewhere the other side of those distant trees. Laura took a fresh grip on his shoulder as he started off. The can swung from his left hand. His right hand rested warily on the gun. He was perpendicular on this world instead of horizontal on another because, on two occasions, his hand had been ready on the gun and because it was the most nervous hand he possessed.

The going was rough. It wasn't so much that the terrain was craggy as the fact that impeding growths got in his way. At one moment he was stepping over an ankle-high shrub, the next he was avoiding a burly plant about to become a tree. Behind the plant would be an entangling creeper, then a natural zareba of thorns, a fuzz of fine moss, followed by a giant fern. Progress consisted of hopping over one item, ducking beneath a second, going around a third and crawling under a fourth.

It occurred to him, belatedly, that if he'd planted the ship tail-first to the lake instead of bow-on, or if he'd let the braking rockets continue to blow after he'd touched down, he'd have saved himself a lot of tedious twisting and dodging. All this obstructing stuff would have been reduced to ashes for at least half the distance to the lake – together with any venomous life it might conceal.

That last thought rang like an alarm-bell in his mind just as he doubled up to pass a low-swinging creeper. On one known planet were creepers that coiled and constricted, swiftly, viciously. Macaws played merry hell if taken within fifty yards of them. It was a comfort to know that this time Laura was riding his shoulder unperturbed – but still he kept his hand on the gun.

The elusive peculiarity of the local vegetation bothered him all the more as he progressed through it. Inability to discover and name this queerness worried him more and more as he went on. A look of self-disgust was on his lean face when he dragged himself free of a clinging bush and sat on a rock in a small clearing.

Dumping the can at his feet he glowered at it and promptly caught a glimpse of something bright and shining a few feet beyond it. He raised his gaze. It was then he saw the beetle.

The creature was the biggest of its kind yet seen by human eyes. There were other things as big, of course, but not of this type. Giant crabs, for instance. But this was no crab. The beetle ambling purposefully across the clearing was large enough to give any crab a severe inferiority complex, but it was a genuine twenty-four carat beetle. And a beautiful one. Like a scarab.

Except that he clung to the irrational notion that little bugs were vicious and big ones companionable, Steve had no phobia about insects. The amiability of large ones was a theory inherited from schoolkid days when he'd been the doting owner of a three-inch stag beetle afflicted with the name of Edgar.

So he knelt beside the creeping monster and placed his hand palm upward in its path. It investigated the hand with waving feelers, climbed onto his palm, paused there ruminatively. It shone with a sheen of brilliant metallic blue and weighed three or four pounds. He jogged it on his hand to judge its weight, then put it down and let it wander on. Laura watched its departure with a sharp, incurious eye.

'*Scarabaeus Anderii*,' concocted Steve, with glum satisfaction. 'I've pinned my name on him – but science will never know it.'

'Dinna fash y'sel'!' bawled Laura in a hoarse voice imported straight from Aberdeen. 'Stop chunnerin', wumman! Y' gie me a pain ahint ma sporran! Dinna – '

'Shut up!' Steve jerked his shoulder, momentarily unbalancing the bird. 'Why do you pick up that barbaric dialect quicker than anything else, eh?'

'McGillicuddy,' shrieked Laura with ear-splitting relish. 'McGilli-Gilli-Gillicuddy! The great black – !' It ended with a word that made Steve's eyebrows shoot up toward his hair and surprised even the bird itself. Filming its eyes in amazement, it tightened its claw-hold on his shoulder, opened the eyes, emitted a couple of raucous clucks and joyfully repeated, 'The great black – !'

It didn't get the chance to complete the new and lovely word. A violent jerk of the shoulder unseated it in the nick of time and it fluttered to the ground, squawking protestingly. *Scarabaeus Anderii* lumbered out from behind a bush, his blue armour glistening as if freshly polished, and stared reprovingly at Laura.

Then something fifty yards away released a snort like the trump of doom and took one step that shook the earth. *Scarabaeus Anderii* scuttled for refuge under a projecting root. Laura made an agitated swoop for Steve's shoulder and clung there desperately. Steve's gun was out and pointing northward before the bird found its perch. Another step. The ground quivered.

Silence for a while. Steve continued to stand like a statue. Then came a monstrous whistle more forceful than that of a locomotive blowing off steam. This was followed by several violent *whufs* then something squat and wide and of tremendous length charged headlong through the half-concealing vegetation while the earth trembled beneath its mass.

Its mad onrush carried it blindly twenty yards to Steve's right, the gun swinging to cover its course but not firing. Steve caught an extended glimpse of a slate-grey bulk, fat-bellied, with a serrated ridge along its back. Despite its pace, the body took quite a time to pass. It seemed several times the length of a fire-ladder.

Bushes were flung roots upmost and trees whipped aside as the creature pounded onward in a straight line which carried it far past the ship and into the dim distance. It left behind a tattered swathe wide enough for a first-class road. Then the reverberations of its mighty tonnage died out and it was gone.

Steve used his left hand to extract a handkerchief and wipe the back of his neck. He kept the gun firmly in his right hand. The explosive shells in that weapon were somewhat wicked; any one of them could deprive an attacking rhinoceros of a hunk of meat weighing two hundred pounds. If a man copped one of them he just strewed himself over the landscape. By what he had seen of that slate-coloured galloper it would need half a dozen shells to feel incommoded. A seventy-five millimetre bazooka would be more effective for kicking it in the back teeth, but probe ships aren't armed with that kind of artillery. Finishing the mopping, Steve replaced the handkerchief and picked up the can.

Laura said pensively, 'I want my mother.'

He offered no reply, feeling that there were times when macaws were conversationally inadequate. Her feathers still ruffled, Laura rode his shoulder and lapsed into surly silence.

The stuff in the lake was water, cold, faintly green and a little bitter to the taste. Coffee would camouflage the flavour. If anything, it might improve the coffee since he liked it to have a decided tang. But the liquid would have to be tested before absorbing it in any quantity. Some poisons were accumulative. It wouldn't do to guzzle gaily while building up a death-dealing reserve of lead or cadmium or anything equally noxious. Filling the freezocan, he lugged it to the ship in easy stages. The swathe helped; it made a convenient path to within short distance of the ship's tail. He was perspiring freely by the time he reached the base of the ladder.

Once inside the vessel he relocked both doors, opened the air-vents, started the auxiliary lighting-set and plugged in the percolator, using water from his badly depleted tank. By now the golden sky had dulled to orange, with purple streamers creeping upward from the horizon. Looking at the scene through the transpex dome, he found that the perpetual haze still effectively concealed the sinking sun. A brighter area to one side was all that indicated its position. He'd need his lights soon.

Pulling out the collapsible table, he jammed its supporting leg into place, plugged into its rim the wooden rod which was Laura's official seat. She claimed the perch at once and watched him beadily as he set out her meal of water, seeds and nuts. Her manners were anything but ladylike and she started eagerly without waiting for him.

A slight scowl lay over his features as he sat at the table, poured out his coffee and commenced to eat. It persisted throughout the meal, was still there when he lay back and gazed speculatively up at the dome.

'I've seen the biggest bug that ever was. I've seen several other bugs. There were a few little ones under a creeper. One was long and brown and many-legged, like an earwig. Another was round and black with red dots on its wing cases. I've seen a tiny yellow spider and a tinier green one of different shape, also a bug that looked like an aphid. But not an ant.'

'Ant,' said Laura. She dropped a piece of oleo nut, climbed down after it.

'Nor a bee.'

'Nor a bee,' echoed Laura, indifferent to the lack. 'Laura loves Steve.'

Still keeping his attention on the dome, he continued musing. 'What's cockeyed about the plants is equally cockeyed about the bugs. I wish I could pin it down. Why can't I? I must be off my head already.'

At that point night fell with a silent bang. The gold and orange and purple abruptly were swamped with a deep, velvety blackness devoid of stars or any random gleam. Except for greenish glowings on the instrument-panel the control-room was Stygian, with Laura swearing steadily on the floor.

Putting out a hand, Steve switched on the indirect lighting. Laura regained her perch, clutching the rescued titbit, concentrated on the job of dealing with it and let him sink back into his thoughts.

'*Scarabaeus Anderii* and some smaller bugs and a few spiders, all different. At the other end of the scale that gigantosaurus. But no ants or bees.' This switch from singular to plural caused a strange twitching in his back hairs. It gave him a peculiar and irrational sense of alarm. In some vague way he felt he had touched right on the heart of the mystery. 'No ant – no ants,' he said. 'No bee – no bees.' Almost he had it – but still it evaded him.

Giving it up for the time being, he cleared the table and did a few minor chores. After that he drew a standard sample from the freezocan and put it through its paces. The bitter flavour he identified as being due to the presence of magnesium sulphate in quantity far too small to prove embarrassing. Drinkable – that was something! Food, drink and shelter were the three essentials of survival. He had enough of the first to last quite a long time. The lake and the ship were his remaining guarantees of life.

He got the logbook and entered the day's report, bluntly, factually, without any embroidery. Partway through he found himself stuck for a name for the planet. *Ander*, he decided, would cost him dear if the millions-to-one chance put him back among the merciless playmates of the Probe Service. It was all right for a bug, not for a planet. *Laura* wasn't appropriate either. Especially when one knew her like he did. It wouldn't be seemly to name a big, golden world after an oversized parrot. Thinking over this golden aspect, he hit on the name of *Oro* and promptly made the christening authoritative by entering it in the log.

By the time he'd finished Laura had her head buried deeply under one wing. Occasionally she teetered and swung erect again. It always fascinated him to see how her balance was maintained even in her slumbers. Studying her fondly, he recalled that unexpected addition to her vocabulary. This shifted his thoughts to a fiery-headed and fierier-tongued individual named Menzies, the sworn foe of a determined arguer called McGillicuddy. If ever the opportunity presented itself, he decided, the educative work of the said Menzies was going to be rewarded with a punch on the nose.

He sighed, put away the log, consulted the ship's mercury-powered chronometer, opened his folding bunk and lay down. One hand switched off the lights. Ten years ago a first landing would have kept him awake all night in dithers of excitement. He'd got beyond that now. He'd done it often enough to have become phlegmatic about it. His eyes closed in preparation for a good night's sleep. He did sleep – for two hours.

What brought him awake within that short time he didn't know but suddenly he found himself sitting bolt upright on the edge of the bunk, his ears and nerves stretched to their utmost, his legs quivering in a way they'd never done before. His whole body fizzed with that queer mixture of palpitation and shock which follows a narrow escape from disaster.

This was something not within his previous experience. Sure and certain in the intense darkness, his hand sought and found the gun. He cuddled its butt in his palm while his mind strained to recall a possible nightmare, though he knew he was not given to frightening dreams.

Laura moved restlessly on her perch, not truly awake yet not asleep, and this was unusual for her.

Rejecting the dream theory, he stood up on the bunk and looked out through the dome. Blackness, the deepest, darkest, most impenetrable blackness it was possible to conceive. And silence, absolute, total. The outside world slumbered in the blackness and the silence as in a sable shroud.

Yet never before had he felt so wide awake and alert in this, his normal sleeping time. Puzzled, he turned slowly around to take in the full circle of unseeable view and at one point he halted. Here, the surrounding blankness was not complete. In the distance far beyond the ship's tail moved a tall, stately glow. Its range was not possible to estimate but the sight of it stirred his soul and caused his heart to leap.

All the same, powerful emotions were now allowed to master his well-disciplined mind. Narrowing his eyes, he tried to discern the nature of the glow while his brain tried to find a reason why the mere sight of it should make him twang like a harp. Bending down, he felt at the head of the bunk, found a leather case, extracted a pair of huge night glasses. The glow was still moving slowly and deliberately, from left to right. He aimed the glasses at it, screwed the lenses into focus and the phenomenon leaped into his vision.

The thing was a great column of golden haze much like that of the noonday sky except that intense gleams of silver and emerald sparkled within it. It was a shaft of glowing, lustrous mist bearing a sprinkling of glittering stars. It was like nothing known to or recorded by any form of sentient life lower than the gods. But was it life itself?

It moved, though its mode of locomotion was not visible. Self-motivation is the prime symptom of life. It could be life, conceivably though not credibly from the Terrestrial viewpoint. Consciously, he preferred to think of it as a strange and purely local appearance similar to the Saharan sand-devil or the Australian willy-willy. Subconsciously, he knew it was life, real life, enormous and terrifying.

He kept the glasses on it while it ceased its rightward movement and slowly receded into the darkness, fore-shortening and increasing distance and gradually fading from view. To the very last the observable field shifted and shuddered as he failed to control the quiver in his hands. And when at last the sparkling haze had gone he sat on the bunk and shivered with an eerie coldness.

Laura was now dodging to and fro along her perch, thoroughly awake and agitated but he wasn't tempted to turn on the lights and make the dome a beacon in the night. His hand went out and felt for her in the darkness. She clambered eagerly onto his wrist, thence to his lap. She was fussy and demonstrative, pathetically yearning for comfort and companionship. He scratched her poll and fondled her while she pressed close against his chest with funny little crooning noises. For some time he soothed her and, while doing so, fell asleep. Laura perched on his forearm, clucked tiredly, put her head under a wing.

There was no further awakening until the outer dark disappeared and the sky again sent its golden glow pouring through the dome. Steve got up, stood on his bunk, had a good look over the surrounding terrain. It remained pre-cisely as it had been the day before. Problems occupied his mind while he prepared their breakfasts; especially that of the weird jumpiness he'd experienced in the night time. Also, Laura was quiet and subdued. Only once before had she been like that – which was when he'd traipsed through the Panplanetary Zoo and had shown her a great crested eagle. Laura had cowered while the eagle stared at her with contemptuous dignity.

Though he had all the time in his life he now felt an urge to hasten. Getting the gun and the freezocan, he made a dozen trips to the lake, wasting no minutes nor stopping to study the enigmatic growths and bugs. It was mid-afternoon by the time he'd filled the ship's fifty gallon reservoir and had the satisfaction of knowing that he'd now got a drinkable quota to match his food supply.

There had been no sign of gigantosaurus or any other animal; for some reason he thought of that creature as an animal rather than a reptile. Once he'd seen something flying in the far distance, birdlike or batlike. Laura had docked a sharp eye at it but betrayed no undue interest. Right now she was far more concerned with a new fruit. Steve sat in the rim of the outer airlock door, his legs dangling, and watched her clambering over a small tree thirty yards away. The gun lay in his lap. He was ready to take a crack at anything that might try to take a crack at Laura.

The bird sampled the tree's crop which resembled blue-shelled lychee nuts. She ate one with relish and grabbed another. Steve lay back in the lock, stretched to reach a bag, then dropped to the ground and went across to the tree. He tried a nut. Its flesh was soft, juicy, sweet and citrous. He filled the bag with the fruit and slung it into the ship.

Nearby stood another tree, not quite the same but very similar. It bore nuts just like the first except that they were larger. Picking one, he offered it to Laura who tried it, spat it out in disgust. She did the same with a second and a third before disregarding further offers. He tasted one himself, licking its flesh gingerly. As far as he could tell it was exactly the same as the smaller nuts. Evidently his taste-buds were misleading; Laura's diagnosis said it was not the same. The difference, much too subtle for him to detect, might be sufficient to ensure a long-drawn and painful end. He flung the nut away, went back to his seat in the lock and ruminated.

That elusive, nagging feature of Oro's plants and bugs could be narrowed down to these two crops of nuts. He felt certain of that. If he could discover why, parrotwise, one nut was edible and the other not, he'd have his finger right on the secret. The more he thought about these similar fruits the more he felt that in sober fact his finger was on the secret already – but he lacked the power to lift it and see what lay beneath.

It was tantalizing, the way his mulling over the subject got him to the same place as before, namely, nowhere. He became annoyed, returned to the trees and subjected them to minute examination. His sense of sight told him that they were individuals of the same species. Laura's sense of whatchamacallit insisted that they were of quite different species. Ergo, one cannot believe the evidence of one's eyes. Of course, he was well aware of that fact since it had long been a platitude of the spaceways. But when you cannot trust your own optics it is legitimate to try to discover why you can't trust them. And he couldn't discover even that.

Tiring of the puzzle, he returned to the ship, locked its doors, called Laura to his shoulder and set off on a tailward exploration. The rules of first landings were simple and sensible. Go in slowly, come out quickly, and remember that all we want from you is evidence of suitability for human life. Thoroughly explore a small area rather than scout a big one; subsequent mapping parties will do the rest. Use your ship as your base and locate it where you can survive; don't move it unnecessarily. Restrict your searches to a radius representing daylight-reach. Lock yourself in after dark.

Was Oro suitable for human life? The unwritten law was that you don't jump to conclusions and say, 'Of course! I'm still living, aren't I?' Cameron, who'd dumped his ship on Mithra, had been convinced that he'd found a new paradise until, on the seventeenth day, he'd discovered the fungoid plague. He'd left like a bat out of hell and had spent many sweaty, swearing days in the Lunar Purification Plant before being considered fit for human society. The authorities had vaporized his ship, rendering it down to its component gases. Mithra had been taboo ever since. Every world was a potential trap baited with scientific delight. The task of the Probe Service was to enter such traps and bounce on the springs. Another dollop of real estate for Terra – if nothing broke one's neck.

Possibly Oro was loaded for bear. The thing that walked in the night bore awful suggestion of non-human power. So did a waterspout. Nobody wins a wrestling match with a waterspout. If this Oro-spout were sentient so much the worse for human prospects. He'd have to get the measure of it, he decided, even if foolhardily he had to chase it through the blank avenues of night. Plodding steadily away from the tail, gun at hand, he mused so deeply that he overlooked the fact that he was not on an authorized search job anyway. Nor did he consider that nothing else remotely human might reach Oro in the next one thousand years. Even space-scouts can be creatures of habit. Their job was to seek out mortal dangers and warn against them; they were likely to continue looking long after the need had passed, long after an alarm can be transmitted.

The ship's chronometer had given him five hours to darkness. Two and a half hours each way; say ten miles outward and ten back. Getting water had consumed his time. On the morrow and henceforth he'd increase the radius to twelve miles and take it easier.

Then all such thoughts fled from his mind as he came to the edge of the vegetation. The stuff did not dribble out of existence with hardy spurs and offshoots fighting for a hold in rocky, infertile ground. It stopped abruptly, in light loam, as if machine-tilled, and from where it ceased spread a different crop. The new growths were tiny and crystalline.

He accepted the crystals without surprise, knowing that novelty is the inevitable feature of any new locale. Things were extraordinary only by Terrestrial standards. Outside of Terra nothing was abnormal or supernormal except insofar as it failed to jibe with its own peculiar conditions. Besides, there were crystalline growths on Mars.

The one hair-raising feature of the situation was the way in which the vegetation growths ended and the crystalline ones began. The borderline was so straight that it gave him a scare merely to see it; a dead-straight cut-off running for miles and miles. It suggested a large-scale cultivation by a colossus. Exactitude of that kind could not be other than artificial. Something – some *thing* – had done it.

Sitting on the heel of his right boot, he examined the crystals and said to Laura, 'Chicken, these things have been planted. Question is: who planted them?'

'McGillicuddy,' suggested Laura, convinced that one name was as good as another.

Putting out a finger he gave a gentle flick at the crystal sprouting near the toe of his boot, a green, branchy object a mere inch in height.

The crystal vibrated and said, 'Zing!' in a sweet, high voice.

He flicked its neighbour and that said, 'Zang!' in a lower tone.

He flicked a third. It emitted no note, but broke into a thousand shards.

Standing up, he scratched his head, making Laura fight for a clawhold within the circle of his arm. One zinged and one zanged and one returned to dust. Two nuts, the same but not the same. Zings and zangs and nuts. The secret was right within the grasp if only he could open his hand and look at what he'd got.

Then he lifted his puzzled gaze and saw something fluttering erratically across the crystal field. It was making for the vegetation. Laura took off with a raucous cackle, her blue and crimson wings beating powerfully. She swooped over the object, frightening it so low that it dodged and side-slipped only a few feet above Steve's head. He saw that it was a large butterfly, frill-winged, almost as gaudy as Laura. The bird swooped again, scaring the insect but not menacing it. He called her back and set out to cross the area in front. Crystals crunched to powder under his heavy boots as he tramped onward.

Half an hour later he was toiling up a steep, crystal-coated slope when his thoughts suddenly jelled and he stopped with such abruptness that Laura spilled from his shoulder and perforce took to wing. She beat around in a circle, came back to her perch, made abusive remarks in an unknown language.

'There's one of this and one of that,' he said. 'No twos or threes or dozens or twenties. Nothing I've seen has repeated itself. There's only one gigantosaurus, only one *Scarabaeus Andreii*, only one of every darned thing. Every item is unique, original, an individual creation in its own right. What does that suggest?'

'I'm not for sale,' reminded Laura.

'For Pete's sake, shut up!'

'For Pete's sake, for Pete's sake!' yelled Laura, much taken by the phrase. 'The great black – !'

Again he upset her balance, making her take a flight while he continued talking to himself. 'It suggests constant and all-pervading mutation. Everything breeds something quite different from itself and there aren't any dominant strains.' He frowned as he realized the snag in this theory. 'But how does anything manage to breed? What fertilizes which?'

'McGilli – ' began Laura, then changed her mind and went quiet.

'Anyway, if nothing breeds true it's going to be tough on the food problem,' he went on, forgetting that giganto-saurus must have solved it somehow. 'What's edible on one plant might be a killer on its offspring. Today's fodder is tomorrow's poison. How's a farmer to know what his crop's going to be? If I am guessing right, this planet won't support a couple of hogs.'

'No, sir. Laura loves hogs.'

'Silence!' he ordered. 'I've just remembered that hundred-ton galloper; a place that shouldn't support a couple of hogs demonstrably does feed that monstrosity and any other fancy animals that may be mooching around. It seems crazy to me. On any planet full of consistent fodder gigantosaurus would thrive. But here, according to my calculations, he's no right to be alive. He should have expired at birth.'

So saying, he topped the rise and found the creature in question sprawling right across the opposite slope. It *was* dead.

The way in which he determined its deadness was swift and effective. Its enormous bulk lay draped across the full length of the slope with its dragonlike head, the size of a lifeboat, pointed toward him. The head had two dull, lacklustre eyes the diameter of beer-barrels. He planted a shell smack in the right eye and a big hunk of noggin promptly flew in all directions. The body did not stir.

There was a shell ready for the other eye should the giant leap to frantic, vengeful life, but the mighty bulk remained supine.

His boots continued to crush crystals as he went down the slope, curved a couple of hundred yards off his route to get round the corpse, and trudged up the farther rise. Momentarily, he wasn't much interested in the dead beast. Time was short and he could come again tomorrow, bringing with him a full-colour stereoscopic camera. Gigantosaurus would go on record in style – but would have to wait.

This second rise was a good deal higher and more trying to climb. Its crest represented the approximate limit of today's expedition, hence he was anxious to surmount it and view the promised land before turning back.

Humanity's urge to see what lay over the hill remained as strong today as back in the dawn of time.

He had to have a look, firstly because elevation gave range to vision, and secondly, because of that scintillating prowler in the night. As nearly as he could estimate, the phenomenon had sunk from sight behind this rise. A column of mist sucked down from the sky might move aimlessly around, going nowhere, but his instinct maintained that this had been no mere column of mist and that it had been going somewhere.

Where?

A little out of breath, he pounded over the crest, looked down into an immense valley and found the answer.

The crystal growths ceased on the crest, again in a perfectly straight line. Beyond them, the light loam, devoid of rock, ran down into the valley and up the farther side. Both slopes were sparsely dotted with queer, jelly-like lumps of matter which lay quivering beneath the sun's golden glow.

From the closed end of the valley jutted a great, glistening fabrication, flat-fronted, with a huge square doorway in its middle. It resembled a tremendous oblong slab of milk-white plastic half-buried endways in a sandy hill. No decoration disturbed its smooth, gleaming surface. No road led to the opening at front. Somehow, it had a new-old air and contrived to look empty while possibly full of anything, including fiends.

Steve's back hairs prickled as he studied this alien erection. One thing was obvious: Oro bore intelligent life. One thing was possible, if not probable: the golden column that had wandered in the night represented that life. One thing was highly likely: fleshy Terrestrials and hazy Orons would have difficulty in finding common basis for friendship and co-operation.

Whereas enmity needs no basis.

Curiosity and caution pulled him opposite ways. One urged him down into the valley while the other tried to drive him back, back, while yet there was time to get away. He consulted his watch. If he started soon, he could make it to the ship before dark. That milky palace was at least two miles away, a good hour's trudging there and back, less if he had to make the return at a top-speed run. Ah, let it wait. Give it another day and he'd have more time available, with the benefit of needful thought between-times.

Caution triumphed. He investigated the nearest jelly-blob. It was flat, slightly domed, green with bluish streaks and many tiny bubbles hiding in its transparency. The thing pulsated. He poked at it with the toe of his boot and it contracted, humping itself in the middle, then sluggishly relaxed. No amoeba, he decided. A low form of life but complicated withal. Laura did not like the object. She skittered off as he bent over it and vented her feelings by bashing a few crystals.

This jelly-blob wasn't exactly like its nearest neighbour nor any of the others. One of each, only one. The same rule applied all along the line: one butterfly of a kind, one bug, one plant, one of these quivering things.

A final stare at the distant mystery in the valley, then he retraced his steps. When the ship came into sight he speeded up like a gladsome voyager nearing home. There were new footprints near the vessel, big, three-toed, deeply impressed spoor which revealed that something large and two-legged had wandered past during his absence. Evidently an animal, for nothing intelligent would have meandered by so casually without circling and inspecting the invader from space. He dismissed it from his mind. There was one and only one whatzit, he felt certain of that.

Once inside the ship he locked the doors, gave Laura a meal, ate his own supper. Then he dug out the log, made his day's entry, had a look around from the dome. Violet streamers again were creeping upward from the horizon. He frowned at the encompassing vegetation. What sort of stuff had bred all this in the past? What sort of stuff would this breed in the future? How did it procreate, anyway?

Wholesale radical mutation suggested modification of genes by hard radiation in persistent and considerable blasts. There shouldn't be much hard radiation on a lightweight planet, not unless it poured down from the sky. Here, it didn't pour from the sky or from any place else. In fact, there wasn't any.

He was pretty certain about this because he had a special interest in it and had taken pains to check up on it. Hard radiation betokened the presence of radioactive elements which, at a pinch, might be usable as fuel. The ship was equipped to detect such stuff. Among his playthings were a cosmic ray counter, a radium hen and a gold-leaf electroscope. So far the counter had registered nothing extraordinary. The hen hadn't given one cluck, in fact the only clucks had been Laura's. He had charged the electroscope on landing and its leaves still strained apart at the horizontal. The atmosphere was dry, ionization negligible, and the leaves didn't look likely to collapse for a week.

'Something's wrong with my theories,' he complained to Laura. 'The gunk in my skull isn't doing its job.'

'Isn't doing its job,' echoed Laura faithfully. She cracked a pecan with a grating noise that set his teeth on edge. 'I tell you it's a hoodoo ship. I won't sail. No, no, not even if you pray for me. I won't, I won't, I won't! Who's drunk?' She grabbed another nut, looked at him beady-eyed. 'Rings bigger than Saturn's. Who's a liar? Yawk! She's down in Grayway Bay on Tethis. Her face is beautiful but her torso more so.'

'You talk too much,' he reproved.

'I'm not for sale,' she gave back. 'Have a nut.'

'Okay,' he accepted, holding out his hand.

Cocking her colourful pate, she inspected his palm, pecked at it, gravely selected a pecan and gave it to him. He broke it and chewed on the kernel while starting up the generator. It was almost as if night were waiting for him. Blackness fell even as he switched on the lights.

With darkness came a keen sense of unease. The dome was the trouble. It blazed like a beacon and there was no way of extinguishing its glare except by turning off the lights. Beacons could attract things. He had no desire to become a centre of attention in present circumstances, that is to say, not at night.

Long experience had bred a lordly indifference to alien animals no matter how peculiar or fierce, but alien intelligences were quite a different proposition. So filled was he with the conviction that the previous night's phenomenon was something that knew its onions that it didn't occur to him to question whether a glowing column had eyes or anything resembling a sense of sight. If he had thought of it he'd have derived no comfort from it. His desire to be weighed in the balance in some eerie, extrasensory manner was even less than his liking for the idea of being examined visually in his slumbers.

An unholy mess of notions and speculations was still brewing in his mind when he turned off the lights, bunked down and went to sleep. Nothing disturbed him this time, but when he awoke with the golden dawn his chest was damp with perspiration and Laura again had sought refuge on his arm.

At breakfast, he said to Laura, 'I'm damned if I'm going to drop dead trying to maintain a three-watch system single-handed, which is what I'm supposed to do if faced by powers unknown and not able to get away. Those armchair warriors at headquarters ought to be given a taste of situations not precisely specified in the book of rules.'

'Burp!' said Laura, with suitable contempt.

'He who fights and runs away lives to fight another day,' Steve quoted. 'It's a Probe Service adage. It's the apex of pure wisdom – when he can run away. We can't.'

'Burrup!' exploded Laura, showing great emphasis.

'For a female your manners are downright disgusting,' he told her. Then he continued, 'I'm not going to spend the brief remainder of my life looking fearfully over my shoulder. The only way to get rid of powers unknown is to convert them into powers known and understood. As Uncle Joe told Willie when dragging him to the dentist, the longer we put it off the worse it'll feel.'

'Dinna fash y'sel',' Laura shouted. 'Burp, gollop, bop!'

He gave her a look of distaste. 'So we'll have a try at tossing the bull. Such a tactic might disconcert the bull more than somewhat.' He grabbed Laura, shoved her into her travelling compartment, slid the panel shut. 'We're going to blow right now.'

Climbing into the control-seat, he stamped on the energizer button. The tail rockets popped a couple of times before breaking into a subdued roar. Juggling the controls to get the preparatory feel of them, he stepped up the boost until the entire vessel trembled and the rear centuris started to glow cherry-red. Slowly the ship commenced to edge its bulk forward and, as it did so, he fed it the take-off shot. A half-mile blast kicked backward and the vessel soared aloft in a shallow curve.

Bringing it around in a wide sweep, he thundered over the borderline of vegetation, the field of crystals and the slope beyond. In a flash he was plunging through the valley, braking rockets flaming from the nose. This was tricky in an area so limited. He had to co-ordinate forward shoot, backward thrust and downward surge, but like most of his kind he took pride in the stunts performable with these vessels. An awe-inspired audience was all he needed to make the exhibition perfect. The vessel landed fairly and squarely on the long, milk-white roof of the alien edifice, slid halfway toward the hill in which it was part-buried, then stopped.

'Man,' he exclaimed, showing total lack of modesty, 'Am I good!' He remained in his seat, gazed around through the dome and wondered whether he ought to add, 'And too young to die.' Occasionally eyeing the chronometer, he waited awhile. The ship must have handed that roof a bang sufficient to wake the dead. If anyone were underneath they'd soon hotfoot out to see who was heaving hundred-ton bottles at their shingles. Nobody emerged. He gave them half an hour in which to react, his hawkish face strained, alert. Nothing happened. Then he gave it up, said, 'Ah, well,' and got out of his seat.

He freed Laura. She waddled out with ruffled dignity like a dowager who has paraded into the men's room. Females were ever curious critters, in Steve's logic, and he ignored her attitude. He claimed his gun, unlocked the doors and dropped down onto the roof. Laura followed reluctantly, came to his shoulder as if thereby conferring a great privilege.

Walking to the edge of the roof, he looked down. The sheerness of the five-hundred-foot drop took him aback. Right below his feet the entrance soared four hundred feet up from ground level and he was standing on the hundred-feet-broad lintel surmounting it. The only way down was to walk to the end of the roof and reach the earthy slope in which it was embedded, seeking a path down that.

He covered a mile to reach the slope, his eyes studying the roof's surface as he progressed and failing to find one crack or joint in the smooth expanse. Huge though it was, the erection appeared to have been moulded all in one piece, a fact that did nothing to lessen inward misgivings. Whoever or whatever created this mighty job weren't pigmies.

From the ground-level the entrance loomed bigger than ever. If there had been a similar gap at the other end of the building, and a clear way through, he could have taken the ship in at one end and out at the other with less difficulty than threading a needle.

Absence of doors didn't seem peculiar. It was hard to imagine any sort of door huge enough to fill this opening yet sufficiently balanced to enable anyone – or anything – to pull open or shut. With a final, cautious look around that revealed nothing moving in the valley, he stepped boldly through the entrance, blinked his eyes, adapted to the lesser light as his visual retention faded and gave up the memory of the golden glow outside.

There was a glow inside, too. But a different one, paler, ghastlier, greenish. It exuded from the floor, the walls, the ceiling, and the total effect of radiation was enough to light the place clearly, with no shadows. He sniffed as his senses took in the scene; there was a strong smell of ozone mixed with other, unidentifiable odours.

To his right and left, rising hundreds of feet, stood great tiers of transparent cases. He went to the ones nearest his right and examined them. They were cubes, each about a yard high, wide and deep, made of something like transpex. Each contained three or four inches of loam from which sprouted a crystal. No two crystals were alike, some small and branchy, others large and indescribably complicated.

Dumb with thought, he went around the back of the monster array and found another behind it, with a thirty-feet gap between the two. Behind that was yet another, similarly spaced. And another and another. All with crystals. The number and variety of the exhibits made his head swirl. He could study only the two bottom rows of each block, but row upon row upon row stepped themselves far above his head and to within short distance of the roof. Their total number was beyond estimation.

It was the same again on the left. Crystals by the thousands. Looking more closely at one especially fine example, he noticed that the front of its case bore a small, near-invisible pattern of dots etched within a lozenge-shaped cartouche. Closer investigation showed that the surfaces of all the cases were similarly marked, differing only in the number and arrangement of dots. Undoubtedly it was some sort of code used for purposes of classification.

'The Oron Museum of Natural History,' he guessed, in a whisper.

'I tell you it's a hoodoo – ' squawked Laura, with some violence, then stopped dumbfounded as her own voice roared through the building in deep, organlike tones. '*Hoodoo . . . hoodoo.*'

'Holy Smoke, will you keep quiet!' hissed Steve. He tried to keep watch on the exit and the interior simultaneously. But the voice rumbled away into the distance without bringing anyone to dispute their trespassing.

He paced hurriedly past the first mountains of tiers to the next array of exhibits. Jelly-blobs in this lot. Small ones no bigger than a wristwatch, numerable in thousands. Nothing showed whether they were alive.

Sections three, four and five took him a mile into the building as nearly as he could estimate. He passed mosses, lichens and shrubs, all apparently dead but wondrously preserved. By this time he was ready to guess at section six – plants. He was wrong. The sixth layout displayed bugs, including moths, butterflies and strange, unfamiliar objects resembling chitinous humming-birds. There was no sample of *Scarabaeus Anderii*, unless it were located a hundred feet up. Or unless an empty box waited for it when its day was done.

Who made these boxes? Had it prepared one for him? One for Laura? He visualized himself, petrified for ever, squatting in the seventieth case of the twenty-fifth row of the tenth tier in section something or other, his front panel duly tagged with its appropriate dots. It was a revolting picture. It gave him the creeps merely to think of it.

Looking for he knew not what, he plunged steadily on, penetrating deeper and deeper into the heart of the building. Not a soul, not a sound, not a footprint. Only that all-pervading smell and the unvarying glow. He had a feeling that the place was visited frequently but never occupied for any worthwhile period of time. Without bothering to stop and look, he passed an enormous case containing a creature faintly resembling a bison-headed rhinoceros, then other still larger cases holding equally larger exhibits, all carefully dot-marked.

Finally, he rounded a box so tremendous that it sat across the full width of the hall. It contained the grandfather of all trees and the great-grandfather of all serpents. Behind, for a change, reared five-hundred-feet high racks of metal cupboards, each with a button set in its polished door, each ornamented with groups of mysteriously arranged dots.

Greatly daring, he pressed the button on a nearby cupboard. Its door slid open with a juicy click. The contents proved disappointing; it was filled with neat stacks of glasslike strips each smothered with dots.

'Super filing-system,' he hazarded. 'Old Professor Junkin would give his right arm to be here.'

'Right arm, right arm,' murmured Laura in a low, faltering voice.

He gave her a sharp look. She was ruffled and fidgety, showing rapidly increasing signs of agitation.

'What's the matter, Chicken?'

She pecked at his ear, turned her anxious gaze the way they had come, side-stepped to and fro on his shoulder. Her neck feathers started to rise; they protruded until they formed a wide collar at the back of her head. A frightened cluck came from her beak and she cowered close against his jacket.

'Damn!' Steve said. He dashed to one side, racing past successive filing-blocks, and got into the ten-yards-wide space between the end block and the wall. His gun was out and he kept watch to the front while his free hand tried to soothe Laura. She snuggled up close, rubbing her head into the soft part of his neck and trying to hide under the angle of his jaw.

'Quiet, Honey,' he whispered. 'Just you keep quiet and stay with Steve and we'll be all right.'

Obediently she was silent but he could feel her starting to tremble. His heart speeded up in sympathy although he could see nothing, hear nothing to warrant it.

Then while he watched and waited, and still in absolute silence, the interior brightness waxed, became less green, more golden. And suddenly he knew what it was that was coming. He *knew* what it was.

He sank to his knees to make himself as small and inconspicuous as possible. Now his heart had started palpitating and no coldness in his mind could freeze it down to slower, more normal beat. The total and awful quietness of the approacher was the unbearable feature. The crushing thud of a weighty foot or hoof would have been better. Colossi have no right to steal along like ghosts.

And the golden glow built up, drowning out the green radiance from floor, walls and roof, setting the multitude of case-surfaces afire with its brilliance. It grew as strong as the golden sky and yet stronger. It became penetrating, all-pervading, unendurable, leaving no darkness in which to hide, no sanctuary for little things.

It flamed like the rising sun or something drawn from the very heart of a sun and the glory of its radiance sent the kneeling watcher's mind awhirl. He struggled fiercely to retain mastery of his brain, to discipline it, to bind it to his will – and failed.

His drawn face beaded with sweat, Steve caught the merest fragmentary glimpse of the column's lower edge appearing between the stacks of the centre aisle. He saw a blinding strip of burnished gold in which glittered a pure white star, then a violent effervescence seemed to occur within his skull and he fell forward into a cloud of tiny bubbles.

Down, down, down he floated through myriad bubbles and swirls and sprays of irridescent froth and foam which shone and changed anew with every conceivable colour.

And all the time his mind strove frantically to battle upward and drag his soul back to the surface.

Deep into the nethermost reaches he sank while still the bubbles swirled around in their thousands and gleamed with numberless hues. Then his progress slowed. Gradually the froth and the foam ceased to rotate upward, stopping its circling, began to turn in the reverse direction. He was rising! He rose for a lifetime, floating weightlessly, in a dreamlike trance.

The last of the bubbles drifted eerily away, leaving him in a brief hiatus of non-existence, then he found himself sprawled full length on the floor with a dazed and shaken Laura clinging to his arm. He blinked his eyes, slowly, several times. They were strained and sore. His heart was still thudding and his legs felt weak. There was an unpleasant sensation in his stomach as if vivid memory had sickened him with a great shock from long, long ago.

He didn't get up from the floor right away; his body was too queasy and his mind too muddled for that. While his wits drifted back and his composure returned, he lay and noted that the invading goldness had gone and that again the interior illumination was a mild, shadowless green. Then his eyes found his wristwatch and he sat up, startled. He'd been flat out for two hours.

With considerable effort he got shakily to his feet. Peering around the end of the huge bank of filing cabinets, he saw that nothing had changed. Instinct or intuition told him that the golden visitor had gone and that once more he had this place to himself. Had the visitor been aware of his presence? Had it made him lose consciousness, or, if not, why had he lost it? Had it done anything about the ship lying in plain sight on the roof?

Picking up his futile gun, he regarded it with contempt before shoving it into his holster. Then he helped Laura onto his shoulder where she clung groggily. After that, he moved deeper into the building.

'I reckon we're safe, Honey,' he told her. 'I think we're too small to be worth anyone's bother. Who goes round killing sparrows when he's got a living to earn? Anyway, the sooner we get the measure of this joint, the better. We've got to learn what we're up against.'

'I won't sail,' declaimed Laura. 'Blow my sternpipes!'

He put the pace on, refusing to admit that his system was jittery with nervous strain or that anything had got him bothered. But he knew he had no desire to encounter that glowing entity again. Once was enough and more than enough. It wasn't exactly that he feared it; it was something else, something he was quite unable to define.

Passing the last bank of cabinets, he found himself facing a machine. It was complicated and bizarre – and it was making a crystalline growth. Near to it another and different machine was manufacturing a horned lizard. There could be no doubt whatever about the process of fabrication because both objects were half-made and both progressed slightly even as he watched. In a couple of hours' time they'd be finished and all they'd need would be . . . would be –

His hair stood up like a stiff brush and he commenced to run. Endless machines, all different, all making different things, plants, bugs, birds, fungoids. It was done by electroponics, atom fed to atom like brick after brick to build a house. It wasn't synthesis because that is assembly and this was assembly plus growth in response to unknown laws. In each and every one of these machines, he knew, was some key or code or cipher, some weird master-control of unimaginable complexity, which determined the precise pattern that each built. And the patterns were infinitely variable.

Here and there assemblies of apparatus stood silent, inactive, their tasks complete. Here and there other monstrous mounds of gadgetry were partly in pieces, either under repair or readied for modification. He stopped momentarily by a machine that had finished its job. It had fashioned a delicately shaded moth which now perched motionless, like a winged jewel, within its fabrication jar. The creature was perfect as far as he could tell. All it was waiting for was . . .

Beads of moisture popped out on his forehead. All that moth needed was the breath of life.

He forced a multitude of wild notions to get out of his mind. It was essential to retain a hold on himself mentally. Divert your attention; take it off this and concentrate on that. Firmly he fastened his attention on one huge, partly disassembled machine lying nearby. Its guts were exposed, revealing great field coils of dull grey wire. Bits of similar wire lay scattered on the floor.

Picking up a short piece, he found it surprisingly heavy. He removed his wristwatch, opened its back, brought the wire near to its works. The Venusian jargoon main bearing fluoresced immediately. V-jargoons invariably glowed in the presence of near radiation. This unknown metal might possibly serve as a fuel. His heart gave a jump of excitement at the mere thought of it.

Should he drag out a big coil and lug it up to the ship? It was very heavy and he'd need a considerable length of the stuff – if it proved usable for his purpose. What if the thieving of the coil caused mousetraps to be set before he returned for a further supply?

It pays to stop and think whenever you've got time to stop and think; that was a fundamental of Probe Service philosophy. Pocketing a sample of the wire, he sought around other disassembled machines for more. The search took him still deeper into the building and he had to fight harder to keep his attention concentrated solely on the task in hand. There was that dog, for instance, standing within its transparent case, statue-like, waiting, waiting. If only it had been anything but recognizably and indisputably an Earth-type dog. It was impossible to avoid seeing it. It would be equally impossible to avoid seeing other, more familiar, more closely related forms – if such were there.

He'd gained seven samples of different radioactive wires when he gave up the hunt. A cockatoo ended his peregrinations. The bird stood unmoving within a jar, its blue plumage smooth and bright, its crimson crest raised, its gleaming eye fixed in what was not death but not yet life. Laura shrieked at it hysterically and the immense hall shrieked back at her with long-drawn howls and moans and rumbles that reverberated into dim distances. Laura's reaction was too much; he wanted no cause for similar reaction of his own.

He sped through the building at top pace, passing the filing cabinets and the mighty array of exhibition cases without a second glance. Bolting through the exit, he climbed the loamy slopes to the roof almost as fast as he'd gone down them. He was panting heavily by the time he reached the ship.

His first action was to check the vessel for signs of interference. There were none. Next, he checked his instruments. The leaves of the electroscope were collapsed. Charging them, he watched them spring open and flop together again. The counter showed radiation aplenty. The hen clucked energetically. He had blundered somewhat; he should have checked them when first he'd landed on the roof. However, no matter. What lay beneath the roof was now known; the instruments would have advised him earlier but not as informatively.

Laura had a feed but her appetite was poor. He kept her company, eating with impatient haste. Then he got out his samples of wire. No two were of the same gauge. One obviously was too thick to enter the feed-holes of the Kingston-Kane motors. It took him half an hour to file it to a suitable diameter. The original piece of dull grey wire took the first test. Inserting it, he set the controls to minimum warming-up intensity, stepped on the energizer-button. Nothing happened.

He scowled to himself. Someday in the far future they might have engines better than the sturdy but finicky Kingston-Kanes, ones that would eat anything eatable from fencing-wire to old boots. Density and radioactivity weren't enough for these motors; the metallic mix had to be right or near enough to rightness to please their bowels.

Going back to the Kingston-Kanes, he extracted the wire, found its end fused into shapelessness. It resembled a dud firework. Definitely a failure. Shoving in the second sample, another grey wire not as dull as the first, he returned to the controls and stamped the energizer. The tail rockets promptly blasted with a low moaning note while the thrust-scale showed sixty per cent normal surge. It wasn't enough.

Some people might have lost their temper at this point. Steve held his down. There was nothing to be gained by biting his knuckles and cursing the heavens. He felt in his pocket, took out the third sample and tested it. No luck. The fourth also was a flop. For reasons at which he couldn't even guess, the fifth produced a peculiar and rhythmic series of blasts that shook the vessel from end to end and caused the thrust-dial needle to waggle wildly between minimum and maximum. He pictured Probe patrols popping through space as though fitted with out-board motors. Anyway, the fifth was no good. He tried the sixth, feeling that luck was running out fast. The sixth belied him; it roared joyously at one hundred and seventy per cent, far in excess of normal thrust. The seventh sample was a flop.

He discarded all but what was left of the sixth wire. It was about twelve gauge, near enough to crawl easily through the feed-conduits. It looked like deep-coloured copper but was harder and heavier. If there were at least a thousand yards of it lying down below, and if he could manage to drag it up and into the ship, and if the golden colossus didn't come along in time to ruin his plans, he *might* be able to blow free. Then he might get somewhere civilized – *if* he could find it. His future was based on an appalling selection of 'ifs.'

The easiest and most obvious way to salvage the needed treasure was to blow a hole in the roof, lower a cable and wind up the wire with the aid of the ship's tiny winch. Problem: how to blow a hole without suitable explosives? The only answer he could find was to drill into the roof, fill the resulting hole with stuff extracted from his ammunition, say a prayer and pop it off electrically. He started to try it but didn't get far. The drill's bit curled up as if gnawing on a diamond. He drew his gun and bounced a shell off the roof. The missile exploded with a hard crack and fragments of shell-casing whined shrilly into the sky. Where it had struck, the roof bore a blast smudge and a couple of fine scratches.

There was nothing for it but to go all the way down and heave on his shoulders as much loot as he could carry. And do it right away. Darkness would fall in due course and he had no desire to encounter the golden thing in the dark. It was fateful enough in broad light of day, or in the queer, green glow of the building's interior, but to have a great unknown stealing silently upon him as he struggled with his plunder through the night was something of which he didn't care to think.

Locking the ship and leaving Laura inside, he returned to the building, hastened to the machine section at back. He stopped to look at nothing on his way. He didn't wish to study anything. The wire was the thing that mattered, only the wire. Mundane thoughts of mundane wire didn't twist one's mind around until one found it hard to concentrate.

All the same, his mind was afire as he searched. Half of it was prickly with alertness, apprehensive of the golden column's sudden return; the other half burned with excitement at the possibility of escape. Outwardly, his manner showed nothing of this; it was calm, assured, methodical.

Within ten minutes he'd found a great coil of the particular metal he was seeking, a huge ovoid, intricately wound, lying beside a partly dismantled machine. He tried to move it but couldn't shift it an inch. The thing was far too big and heavy for one man to handle. To get it onto the roof he'd have to cut it up *in situ* and make several trips of it. To make matters worse, some of its inner windings were fused together. So near and yet so far! Freedom depended upon his ability to move a quantity of wire five or six hundred feet vertically. He muttered some of Laura's words to himself.

Although the wire-cutters were ready in his hand, he paused to think, decided to look farther before tackling this difficult job. It was a wise move that brought prompt reward for at a point a mere hundred yards away he came across another, smaller coil, wheel-shaped, in good condition, easy to unreel. Even this one was much too heavy to carry but with a tremendous effort that made his muscles crack he got it up on its rim and proceeded to roll it along like a monster tyre.

Several times he had to stop and let the coil lean against the nearest stack of cases while he took a breather. One case shook under the impact of the coil and its shining, spidery occupant stirred in momentary simulation of life. His dislike of the spider increased with its motion. He made his pause brief, then bowled the coil onward.

Purple streaks again were creeping from the horizon when he rolled his loot out of the huge exit and reached the bottom of the earthy bank. Here he stopped, clipped at the wire with his cutters, took firm grip on a free end and climbed the bank with it. The wire uncoiled without hindrance until he reached the ship where he attached it to the winch, wound the lot in and rewound it on the feed spool.

Night fell in one ominous swoop. His hands were trembling slightly but his lean face was expressionless, phlegmatic, as he carefully threaded the wire's end through the automatic injector and into the feed-hole of the Kingston-Kanes. That done, he slid open Laura's door, gave her some of the fruit they'd picked from the Oron tree. She accepted it morbidly, her manner subdued and not inclined for speech.

'Stay inside, Chicken,' he soothed. 'With luck, we're getting out of here and going home.'

Shutting her in, he climbed into the control-seat, switched on the nose-beam, saw it pierce the darkness and light up the facing cliff. Then he stamped on the energizer and warmed-up the tubes. Their bellow was violent and comforting. At thrust seventy per cent better than normal he'd have to be very careful in all his adjustments; it wouldn't do to melt his tail off just when success was within his grasp. All the same, he felt strangely impatient, as if every minute counted, aye, every second.

But he contained himself, got the venturis heated, gave a couple of discreet puffs on his starboard steering flare, watched the cliff sideways as the ship slewed around on its belly. Another puff and another and he had the ship nose-on to the front edge of the roof. There seemed to be a faint aura visible in the gloom far ahead and he switched off the nose-beam to see it better.

It was a yellow haze shining over the rim of the opposite slope. Electric thrills ran through his scalp as he looked at it. The haze strengthened and rose higher. His eyes strained into the outer pall as he watched it fascinatedly and his hands were frozen on the controls. There was dampness exuding on his back. Laura was completely silent, not even shuffling uneasily as was her wont. He wondered if she were cowering.

With a mighty effort of will he shifted the control a couple of notches, lengthened the tail-blast. Trembling in its entire fabric, the ship edged forward. Summoning all he'd got, Steve forced his reluctant hands to administer the take-off boost. With a tearing crash that thundered back from the cliffs the little vessel leaped outward and upward on an arc of fire. Peering through the transpex, Steve caught a fragmentary and foreshortened glimpse of the great golden column advancing majestically over the crest, the next instant it had dropped behind his tail and his bow was arrowing for the stars.

An immense relief flooded through his soul though he knew not what there had been to fear. But the relief was there and so great was it that he worried not at all about whence he was bound or for how long. Somehow he felt certain that if he swept onward in a great cosmic curve he'd pick up a Probe beat-note sooner or later. Once he got a beat-note from any source at all, it would lead him out of the celestial maze.

Luck remained with him and his optimistic hunch proved correct, for while still among completely strange constellations he caught the faint throb of Hydra 111 on his twenty-seventh day of sweep. That throb was his lighthouse beckoning him home.

He let go a wild shriek of, 'Yippee!' thinking that only Laura could hear him. But he was heard elsewhere.

Down on now faraway Oro, deep in the monster workshop, the golden giant paused blindly, as if listening. Then it slid stealthily along the immense aisles, reaching the filing system. A compartment opened. Two glassy plates came out.

For a moment the plates contacted the Oron's strange, sparkling substance, became etched with an array of tiny dots. They were returned to the compartment and the door closed. The golden glory with its imprisoned stars then glided quietly back to the machine section.

Something near to the gods had scribbled its notes. Nothing lower in the scale of life could have translated them or deduced their full import.

In simplest sense, one plate may have been inscribed, 'Biped, erect, pink, homo intelligens type P.739, planted on Sol 111, Condensation Arm BDB – moderately successful.'

Similarly, the other plate may have recorded, 'Flapwing,

large, hook-beaked, vari-coloured, periquito macao type K.8, planted on Sol III, Condensation Arm BDB – moderately successful.'

But already the sparkling hobbyist had forgotten his brief notes. He was breathing his essence upon a jewelled moth.

THE MECHANICAL MICE

It's asking for trouble to fool around with the unknown. Burman did that. Hence, a lot of people now hate anything that clicks, ticks, emits whirring sounds or generally behaves like an asthmatic alarm-clock. They've got mechanophobia. Dan Burman gave it to them.

Who hasn't heard of the Burman Bullfrog Battery? The very same chap! He puzzled it out from first to last and topped it with its world-wide slogan: Power In Your Pocket. It was no mean feat to concoct a thing the size of a trouser-button that could pour out as much energy as a couple of heavy duty car batteries. Burman differed from everyone else in thinking that it was a mean feat.

Burman looked me over very carefully, then said, 'When that technical journal sent you around to see me twelve years ago you listened sympathetically. You didn't treat me as if I were an idle dreamer or a congenital idiot. You gave me a decent write-up and started the flood of publicity that eventually made me a stack of money.'

'It wasn't because I loved you,' I assured. 'It was because I was satisfied that your gadget really worked.'

'Maybe.' He eyed me in the speculative manner of one about to produce a rabbit from a hat and uncertain of the reaction. 'We've been pally since that time and we've filled in some idle hours together. I feel that you are friend enough to listen to a seemingly silly confession.'

'Get it off your chest,' I encouraged. We had become friends, as he'd said. It was merely that we'd taken a liking to each other, found each other congenial. He was a brainy character, Burman, a definite egg-head, but there was nothing of the pedantic professor about him. Fortyish and slightly florid, normal looking and neatly dressed, he might have been a prosperous estate agent or a fashionable dentist, to judge by appearances.

'Bill,' he said. 'I didn't invent that battery.'

'Somebody did,' was all I could think to say, 'even if you snatched the credit and the profits.'

'I stole the idea,' he insisted. 'It was a blatant theft. Furthermore, I didn't know at the time what I was stealing. If you think that's crazy then listen to this: I don't know whence I stole it.'

'Your conscience must be killing you,' I offered.

He disregarded that remark and went on. 'That's not the end of it. It's merely the beginning. After ten years of careful, exacting work I've invented or built or stolen another contraption. It must be the most complicated thing in creation.' He banged a fist on his knee and his voice rose complainingly. 'And now that I've completed it I don't know what I've made.'

'Surely when an inventor experiments he knows what he's doing?'

'He half-knows or quarter-knows,' said Burman. 'And if he's a nuthead he may even be lunging in the dark. I've invented only one thing in my life and that was more by accident than good judgment, the way many basic discoveries have been found. My trouble is that I got hold of something that leads to others.'

'Don't they all? Somebody found that rubbed amber picked up dust and umpteen years later we got colour television. I fail to see – '

'You will see more if you listen more,' he chided. 'I got

hold of one thing that was the key to others. It gave me the battery. It had nearly given me things of far greater importance. On several occasions it has almost but not quite placed within my inadequate hands and half-understanding mind things that would alter this world out of recognition.' He leaned forward and poked at me to lend emphasis to his speech. 'Now it has given me a mystery that has cost me ten years of intensive work and a large sum of money. I finished it last night. It's done, it's complete — and I don't know what it is.'

'Perhaps if I had a look at it —'

'Just what I'd like you to do.' He switched to pardonable enthusiasm. 'It's a beautiful piece of work even though I say so myself. But you need an exceptional imagination to figure out what it is and what it's supposed to do.'

'Assuming that it can do something,' I said.

'Yes,' he agreed, 'if it can. But I'm positive it has a function of some kind.' Getting up, he opened a door. 'Come on.'

It was more of a spectacle than King Tut's coffin. It was a large metal box with a glossy rhodium-plated surface. In general size and shape it did bear faint resemblance to an upended sarcophagus and had the same brooding, ominous air of a burial casket waiting for its future owner to give up the ghost.

There were a couple of small glass windows in its front through which could be seen a multitude of wheels as beautifully finished as those in an expensive watch. Elsewhere, several tiny lenses stared with sphinxlike indifference. There were three small trapdoors on one side, two on the other and a large one at the front. From the top two knobbed rods of metal stuck up like a goat's horns, adding a satanic touch to the thing's vague air of waiting for midnight burial.

'It's an automatic layer-outer,' I suggested, viewing the gadget with frank distaste. I pointed to one of the trapdoors.

'You shove the shroud in there and the lace collar in here and the corpse comes out the other side with its hair brushed, wearing a happy smile, reverently composed and ready wrapped.'

'So you don't like its looks either,' remarked Burman. He dragged open a drawer in a nearby tier, took out a mass of drawings. 'These are its insides. It has various electronic circuits complete with coils, condensers, transistors, solenoids, the lot. There's also something I can't quite understand but might be a tiny laser-activated furnace. There are also mechanical parts I recognize as cog-cutters and pinion-shapers. It embodies several small-scale multiple stampers apparently for dealing with sheet metal. There are vague suggestions of an assembly-line ending in that compartment shielded by the door in front. Have a look at the drawings yourself. You can see the whole thing's an extremely complicated device for manufacturing something little less complicated.'

The plans showed him to be correct. But they didn't show everything. Any efficient machine designer could have deduced the gadget's function if given complete details. The details were far from complete. Burman admitted this, saying that he had made some parts 'on the spur of the moment' while others he had been 'impelled to manufacture.' Short of pulling the whole machine to pieces there was enough data to whet the curiosity but not sufficient to satisfy it.

'Start the damn thing and see what it does.'

'I'm way ahead of you with that idea,' Burman said. 'I've tried. It won't start. There's no starting-handle or switch or anything to suggest how it might be started. I tried everything I could think of, without result. One of the main circuits ends in those antenna at the top and I even applied current to those but nothing happened.'

'Maybe it's a self-starter,' I ventured. Then a thought struck me and I added, 'Timed.'

'Eh?'

'Set for an especial time. When the dread moment arrives it'll go off of its own accord, like a bomb.'

'Don't be so melodramatic,' said Burman, uneasily. Bending, he peered into one of the tiny lenses. He appeared to be challenging his own creation eyeball to eyeball.

'Bz-z-z!' murmured the contraption in a faint undertone that was almost inaudible.

Burman jumped a foot. Then he backed away, eyed the thing warily, glanced at me.

'Did you hear what I heard?'

'Sure did.' Finding the drawings, I mauled them around. The little lens took a bit of tracing but it was there all right. It had a selenium cell behind it. 'An optic,' I said. 'It saw you and reacted. So it isn't dead, even if it does just stand there seeing no evil, hearing no evil, speaking no evil.' I put a white handkerchief against the lens.

'Bz-z-z!' repeated the coffin on a slightly higher note.

Taking the handkerchief, Burman placed it against the other lenses. Nothing happened. Not a sound was heard, not a funeral note. Just nothing.

'It beats me,' he confessed.

By this time I'd got a bit fed up. If the lunatic article had performed, in any manner at all, I'd have written it up and perhaps started another financial snowball rolling for Burman's benefit. But there's nothing sensational about a casket that makes a noise whenever it feels temperamental. A mere buzz-box isn't news. The time had come when firm treatment was needed.

'You've been happily mysterious about how you got hold of this brainwave in the first place,' I told him. 'Why can't you go to the same source for information about what it's supposed to be?'

'I'll tell you – or, rather, I'll show you.'

From his big wall-safe Burman took a steel box and from the box he produced a gadget. This one was far smaller and simpler than the useless mass of works under discussion. It looked very much like one of those ancient crystal sets except that the crystal was the size of a golf-ball and was set inside a horizontal vacuum-tube. But there was the same cat's whisker and the same single tuning-dial. Attached to the lot by a length of flex was what might have been a pair of headphones except that in place of the phones were a pair of smoothly rounded copper hemispheres large enough to fit over the ears and tight against the skull.

'My one and only invention,' informed Burman with a touch of pride.

'What is it?'

'A time-travelling device.'

The laugh with which I responded was sour. I had read about such things. In fact, I had written about them. They were nonsense. Nobody could travel through time either forward or backward. It was a physical impossibility.

'Let me see you go hazy and vanish into the future.'

'I'll show you something very soon,' Burman answered with an assurance I didn't like. He said it with the positive air of a man who knows darned well that he really can do something that everyone else knows darned well cannot be done. He pointed at the crystal set. 'It wasn't perfected at the first attempt. Thousands of others must have tried and failed. I was the lucky one whose number came out of the hat. I must have chosen a peculiarly individualistic crystal. I still don't know how it does what it does. I've never been able to repeat its performance even with a crystal apparently identical.'

'And it enables you to travel in time?'

'Only forward. It won't take me backward, not even as much as one day. But it can carry me forward an immense distance, perhaps to the very crack of doom, perhaps everlastingly through infinity.'

I had him there. I'd got him firmly entangled in his own absurdities.

'You say you can travel forward but not backward, not

even by one day. Then how can you return to the present once you've gone into the future?'

'The answer is childishly simple,' he gave back. 'I never leave the present. I don't partake of the future, play any part in it, have any influence upon it. I merely survey it from the vantage point of the present. All the same, it is time-travel in the correct sense of the term.' He seated himself and continued. 'Think, Bill. What *are* you?'

'Who, me?'

'Yes, you. What are you?' He went on to provide the answer. 'Your name is Bill. You're a body and a mind. Which of them is Bill?'

'Both,' I said, positively.

'True – but they're different parts of you. They are not the same even though they go around together like Siamese twins. Now, your body moves always in the present, the dividing-line between past and future. But your mind is not so tied, it is more free. It can think and is in the present. It can remember and at once is in the past. It can imagine and is in the future, in its own choice of all possible futures. Your mind can travel through time and it's done it so often you haven't even noticed it.'

It was fair reasoning. Fundamentally he was right in saying that anyone could travel through time, backward or forward, within the limits of his own memory and imagination. At that very moment I could go back twelve years and see him in my mind's eye as a younger man, smoother faced and darker haired. The picture was as perfect as my memory was excellent. For that brief spell I was twelve years back in all but flesh.

'I call this thing a psychophone,' Burman went on. 'When you try to imagine what the future will be like you make a characteristic choice from all the logical possibilities, you pick your personal favourite from a number of likely futures. The psychophone somehow – heaven alone knows how – tunes its user into future *reality*. It compels him to depict with his own mind the future as it will be shaped in actuality, eliminating all the various alternatives that for one reason or another will not occur.'

'An imagination-simulator, a dream-machine,' I scoffed. 'How can you be certain that it's giving you the real thing?'

'Because it's consistent,' he replied. 'It repeats the same features, the same trends, the same details far too often for the whole lot to be dismissed as mere coincidence. Besides, I got the battery from the future. It works, doesn't it?'

'It does. Nobody can deny that you picked a winner from somewhere. Well, if you can travel in time, so can I. How about letting me have a go? Another pair of eyes might notice evidence that you've missed and thus help with the problem.'

'I'm still way ahead of you,' commented Burman, smiling. 'I called you round in the hope of persuading you to take part in this imbecility.' He pulled a chair into position. 'Sit here and have your own snoop into the future.'

Clipping the headband over my skull and fitting the copper cups against my ears, Burman connected his contraption to the mains and switched it on or did some twiddling that presumably was a form of switching on.

'All you have to do,' he said, 'is close your eyes, compose yourself and let your mind wander free.'

He meddled with the cat's whisker and said, 'Ah!' a couple of times. Each time I got a peculiar dithery feeling in my cranium. When he drew it out to, 'Ah-h-h!' I played sneaky and took a peep beneath lowered lids. The crystal was glowing like a strange god's eye in a long forgotten temple. A menacing crimson.

Closing my optics, I let my mind run loose as per instructions. Something was flowing between the copper electrodes, a queer, indescribable something that felt with stealthy fingers at a secret portion of my brain. I developed the crazy notion that they were the dextrous digits of a yet-to-be-born magician who was going to shout, 'Hey, presto!'

and pull my entire lump of think-meat out of a weird-looking hat — assuming that they'd be wearing hats in the thirtieth or fiftieth century.

What was it like, or rather what would it be like in the faraway future? Would there be retrogression? Would humanity again be composed of scowling, fur-kilted creatures lurking in caves? Or had progress continued — perhaps even to the development of men like gods?

Then it happened. I pictured quite voluntarily a ferocious-looking half-ape immediately followed by a huge-domed superman with glittering eyes, the latter being my version of the ugliness we hope to attain. Right in the middle of this erratic dreaming the intruding fingers warped my brain, dissolved my phantoms and replaced them with a dictated picture that I witnessed with all the helplessness and clarity of a nightmare.

I saw a fat man orating. He was quite an ordinary individual as far as looks went, in fact he was so normal that he appeared henpecked. But he was attired in a Roman toga and wore a small black box where his laurel wreath ought to have been. His audience was similarly dressed and all of them were adorned with boxes, like a convention of fish-porters. What Fatty was saying was obscure but he said it as if he meant it.

The crowd was in the open air with great curved rows of seats visible in the background. Presumably an outside auditorium of some sort. Judging by the distance of the back rows it must have been of tremendous size. Far behind its sweeping ridge a great edifice jutted into the sky, a cubical erection with walls of glossy squares, like an immense glasshouse.

'Fwot?' bellowed Fatty with much heat. 'Wuk, wuk, wuk, morna noona ni. Bok onned, ord this, ord that.' He stuck an indignant finger against the mysterious object on his pate. 'Bok onned, wuk, wuk, wuk. Fwot?' He glared around. 'Fnix!' The crowed shifted uneasily and murmured timid approval but this feeble support was enough for

Fatty. Making up his mind, he flourished a plump fist and shouted, 'T'ell wit'm!' Then he tore his box from his head.

A moan of sheer horror went up from the crowd and nobody moved. Dumb and wide-eyed, they stood and stared as if paralysed by the sight of a human being sans box. Something with a long, slender, streamlined body and broad wings soared upward in the distance, bulleted nearer and swooped over the auditorium. Still the crowd did not move.

His face suffused with triumph, Fatty bawled, 'Lem see'm make wuk now! Lem see'm – '

He got no further. With a rush of mistiness from its tail, but in perfect silence, the soaring thing hovered and sent down a spear of faint silvery light. The beam touched Fatty. He rotted where he stood, like a victim of superfast leprosy. He rotted, collapsed, crumbled within his sagging clothes, became dust as once he had been dust. It was horrible.

The concourse of watchers did not flee in panic. Not one expression of fear or revulsion came from anyone's lips. They stood there, without a sound, staring, just staring like a horde of wooden dummies. The thing in the sky circled to survey its handiwork then dived low over the mob, a stubby antenna in its prow sparking furiously. As one man, the crowd made a left turn. As one man it commenced to march, left, right, left, right.

Tearing off the headband, I told Burman what I had seen or what his gadget had persuaded me to think I had seen.

'Automatons,' he said. 'Glassite skyscrapers and reactionships.' He thumbed through a big diary filled with notations in his own hand. 'Yes, you were very early in the thirtieth century. Unrest was persistent for twenty years prior to the Antibox Rebellion.'

'What rebellion?'

'The Antibox, the revolt of the automatons against the thirtieth century Technocrats. Jackson-Dkj–99717, a cunning and successful schemer with a warped box, secretly warped hundreds of other boxes and eventually led the rebels to victory in 3047. A century later his great grandson, a greedy, thick-headed individual, caused the rebellion of the Boxless Freemen against his own clique of Jacksocrats.'

I gaped at this recital. 'The way you tell it makes it sound like history.'

'Of course it's history,' he asserted. 'History that is yet to be.' He was pensive for a while. 'Studying the future will seem a weird process to you. But one can get accustomed to anything. It's now quite a normal procedure to me. I've been doing it for years and, in a way, familiarity has bred contempt. The big difficulty is that selectivity isn't as good as it ought to be. One can pick on some especial period twenty times in succession only to find oneself each time in a different month or even a different year. In fact one is fortunate to strike twice in the same decade. Hence, my data is very erratic.'

'I can well imagine. A good guesser might guess the correct time to within a minute or two but never to the second.'

'Quite!' he responded. 'So the hell of it is that mine's been the privilege of watching the panorama of the future but in a manner so sketchy that I've been unable to grasp its best prizes. Once I was lucky enough to witness a twenty-fifth century power-pack being assembled from first to last. I got every detail down before I lost the scene which I've never been able to hit on again. I made that power-pack and you know the result.'

'So that's how you concocted the battery?'

'It is. But mine, good as it may be, is not as good as the one I saw. An essential detail is missing and I cannot imagine what it can be.' Then he added, 'I was most painstaking about getting that data. I could have sworn I'd got all of it. Yet I didn't. I suspect I missed something because I had to miss it.'

'What d'you mean?'

'History, past or future, permits no glaring paradox. Having snatched a technical development from the twenty-fifth century, I am recorded in that age as the twentieth century inventor of the thing. In the intervening five centuries they've improved the Burman Battery. Automatically, that improvement has been withheld from me. Future history is as fixed and unalterable as past history. Neither can be changed by the present.'

'So it seems,' I said. 'Explain to me this fancy coffin that does nothing but go *bz-z-z*.'

'Dammit!' exploded Burman, 'that's just what's driving me crazy. It can't be a paradox, it just can't.'

'So – ?'

'It must be a seeming paradox.'

'All right. You tell me how to market a seeming paradox and the commercial uses thereof and I'll give it a first-class write-up.'

Ignoring the sarcasm, he went on, 'I tried to probe the future as far as a human mind can go. In the end I saw nothing, nothing but the vastness of a sterile floor upon which sat a huge machine gleaming in silent, solitary majesty. Somehow, it seemed aware of my scrutiny across the gulf of ages. It held my attention with a power almost hypnotic. For more than a day, for a full thirty-six hours I kept full attention on that vision without losing it. It was by far the longest time I have retained a future scene.'

'Did this machine do anything?'

'It made no visible motions, if that's what you mean. But I wouldn't swear that it did nothing. I suspect it of having influenced me to draw. For long, tiring hours I worked like mad making drawings with all the confidence of a skilled draughtsman. Its insides could not be seen but somehow they came to me, somehow I knew them. I drew and drew with the frenzy of one who works against time, anxious to capture the details before they vanished for ever. I lost the scene at four o'clock in the morning and found myself with a stack of complicated drawings, heavy-lidded eyes, a thumping headache and a half-scared feeling attributable to I knew not what.' He went silent for a short time. 'A year later I plucked up courage and started to construct the thing I had drawn. It's cost me enough time and money to have me certified as mentally unbalanced. But I completed it. It's finished.'

'And all it does is buzz,' I remarked with sympathy.

'Yes.' He let go a sigh.

There was nothing more to be said. Burman gazed moodily at the wall, miserable in defeat. I fiddled aimlessly with the copper ear-pieces of the psychophone. My imagination was as good as anyone's but for the life of me I could neither imagine nor suggest a profitable market for a metal whatzit filled with watchmaker's junk. No, not even if it did make odd noises.

A faint, smooth *whirr* came from the coffin. It was a new sound that startled us as much as a sudden shot. *Whirr-r-r!* it went again. Finely machined wheels spun behind the window in its front.

'It's coming into action,' said Burman, voicing the obvious as though reluctant to believe it.

Bz-z-z! Whirr-r-r! The whole affair suddenly slid sideways on its hidden castors.

The devil you know is less frightening than the devil you don't. This sudden demonstration of life and motion didn't really scare us but it certainly made us feel leery. The coffin-thing might well be the devil we didn't know. So we stood there gazing fascinatedly and feeling apprehensive of we knew not what.

Movement ceased after the thing had glided four or five feet. It stood there, silent, imperturbable, its front lenses eyeing us with glassy lack of expression. Mutual contemplation lasted several minutes before the contraption slid another couple of feet. More pointless staring. Then a swifter slide that brought it right up against the laboratory table. Here it stopped and began to emit synchronized ticks like those of a couple of sympathetic grandfather clocks.

Burman exclaimed, 'Something's going to happen.'

If the machine could have spoken it would have taken the words right out of his mouth. He'd hardly voiced his prophecy when a trapdoor in the coffin's side fell open, a jointed metal arm shot out and snatched at a marine chronometer lying on the table.

With a surprised oath, Burman jumped forward to rescue the instrument. He was too late. The arm got it, whipped it into the machine, the trapdoor shut with a hard snap like the vicious clash of a sprung bear-trap. Simultaneously, another trapdoor in the front fell open, another jointed arm shot out and in again, spearing with ultra-rapid motion almost too fast to follow. That trapdoor also snapped shut, leaving Burman gaping down at a torn waistcoat from which his expensive watch and equally expensive gold chain had been ripped away.

'Hell!' he said, backing off to a safe distance.

'It's got an appetite for timepieces,' I offered, 'or for the works inside them.'

We stood looking warily at the machine while we tried to think what to do for the best. It didn't move again, just posed there ticking steadily as if ruminating upon a welcome meal. Its lenses gazed at us with all the tranquil disinterest of a well-fed cow happily digesting a mess of cogs, pinions and toothed wheels.

Because its subtle air of menace seemed to have faded away, or because we sensed its total preoccupation with its own digestive processes, we made an effort to recover Burman's valuable watch and chain. Burman tugged mightily at the trapdoor through which the loot had vanished but failed to move it. I had a try, with no better result. The door was sealed as solidly as if welded in. A large screwdriver failed to pry it open. A crowbar or a good jemmy might have done the job but at that point

Burman decided he didn't want to damage the machine which, after all, had cost him far more than the lost watch.

Tick-tick-tick! went the coffin stolidly. We were back where we'd started, playing with our fingers and not one whit wiser than before. Short of wrecking it, there was nothing we could do and the contraption knew it. So it posed there, staring blankly through its lenses, and jeered *tick-tick-tick!* From its belly, or where its belly should have been if it'd had one, a slow warmth radiated. According to Burman's drawings, that was where the tiny electric furnace was located.

The thing was functioning, there could be no doubt of that. We were far from happy about the fact. There we stood, like a couple of bemused yokels at a side-show of a country fair, not knowing what the machine was supposed to do and all the time it was doing it under our very eyes.

From where was it drawing its power? Were that pair of antenna sticking like horns from its head busily sucking current from the atmosphere? Was it feeding off broadcast radiation? Or did it have an internal supply of its own? All the visible evidence suggested that it was doing something, perhaps making something, perhaps scheming to give birth to something, but to what?

Tick-tick-tick! was the only reply.

Questions were still unanswered, curiosity remained unsatisfied and the machine was still ticking industriously at the hour of midnight. We couldn't stand waiting there for ever. Perforce we surrendered the problem until next morning. Burman locked and double-locked his laboratory before we left.

Police Officer Matthew's job was not a complicated one. All he had to do was amble cautiously around three or four blocks, keeping a wary eye on stores in general and the big jeweller's shop in particular, phoning headquarters once per hour from the post on the corner.

Night work suited Matthew's taciturn disposition. He

could wander along communing with himself and there
was little to divert him from his inward ruminations. In his
particular section nothing ever happened at night, nothing.
To his way of thinking, he had the softest and easiest
patrol in the whole town.

Stopping outside the jeweller's gem-bedecked window,
he gazed through the thick glass and the heavy grille
behind it to where a forty-watt bulb shed light over a
massive safe. There was a rajah's ransom inside that steel
box. The guard, the grille, the automatic alarms and
sundry ingenious traps preserved it from the inquisitive
fingers of anyone who wanted to ransom a rajah. Nobody
had made the brash attempt in twenty years. Nobody had
so much as made a try for the contents of the window.

He glanced upward at a faintly luminescent patch of
cloud behind which lay the hidden moon. Turning, he
strolled on. A prowling cat sneaked past him, treading
softly and silently, hugging the angle of the wall. His sharp
eyes detected its shape even in the night-time gloom but he
ignored it and continued to the corner.

The cat turned back, came below the window through
which he had stared. It stopped, one forefoot half-raised,
its ears cocked forward. Then it flattened belly-low against
the concrete, its burning orbs wide, alert, intent. Its tail
waved slowly from side to side.

Something small and bright came skittering toward it,
moving with mouselike speed and agility close to the angle
of the wall. The cat tensed as the object came nearer.
Suddenly the thing was within range and the cat pounced
with lithe eagerness. Hungry claws dug at a surface that
was not soft and furry but hard and bright and slippery.
The thing darted around like a clockwork toy as the cat
tried in vain to hold it. Finally, with an angry snarl, the cat
swiped at it viciously, knocking it a couple of yards where
it rolled onto its back and emitted protesting clicks and
tiny, urgent impulses that its feline attacker could not
sense.

Gaining the gutter with a single bound, the cat crouched again. Something else was coming. The cat muscled and its eyes glowed. Another object slightly similar to the one just attacked, but a little bigger, a fraction noisier and much different in shape. It resembled a small gold-plated cylinder with a conical front from which projected a single blade and it sped vengefully along on concealed wheels.

Again the cat leaped. Down on the corner Matthew heard a brief flurry that included a couple of yowls and ended in a shriek and a gargle. The sounds did not bother him; he'd heard cats and rats and other vermin make all sorts of queer noises in the night. Phlegmatically, he continued on his beat.

An hour later Police Officer Matthew had worked his way around to the fateful spot. Aiming his flashlamp at the body, he rolled the corpse over with his foot. The cat's throat had been cut with a savagery that almost decapitated it. He scowled down at it. He was no lover of cats himself but he didn't approve of one being kicked, much less slashed.

'Somebody,' he muttered, 'needs beating up!'

His big foot shoved the dead animal back into the gutter whence street cleaners would cart it away in the morning. He turned his attention to the window and saw the light still shining on the untouched safe. His mind was still on the cat while his eyes looked in and insisted that something was wrong. Then he dragged his thoughts back to business, alerted his scrutiny, realized what was wrong and sweated with shock.

In the centre of the window the serried trays of rings still gleamed undisturbed. To the right the display of silverware shone as before. But on the left had been an array of very expensive watches. They were no longer there, not one of them. Their glass stands and velvet-lined cases stood empty. He remembered that in the front had rested a beautiful calendar-chronometer priced at a year's salary. That, too, was absent from parade.

The beam of his flash trembled as he tried the gate, found it fast, secure. The door behind it was firmly locked. The transom was closed, its heavy wire guard tightly in place. He took a closer look at the window and soon found a neat, circular hole about three inches in diameter, right down in one corner on the side nearest the missing items.

Matthew's curse was explosive as he bolted to the telephone. His hand shook with indignation when it took up the ear-piece. Getting headquarters, he recited his story. He thought he knew how it had been done, having once read of a similar trick being pulled elsewhere.

'Looks as if they cut a disc with a rotary diamond, lifted it out with a suction-cup, then fished through the hole with a telescopic rod.' He listened a moment. 'Yes, yes, that's what gets me – the rings must be worth ten times as much.'

His gaze examined the street while he paid attention to the voice at the other end of the line. Soon his eyes found another shape lying in the gutter. He told the telephone to hold on while he went for a look. Another dead cat. Same as the previous one. Ear to ear. He returned and shouted along the line, 'What's more, some maniac's sneaking around slaughtering cats.'

Replacing the phone, he hurried back to the maltreated window, stood guard in front of it until a police car rolled up. Four men piled out of it.

The first said, 'Cats! I'll say somebody's got it in for cats! We passed two farther back. They were lying in the middle of the road, right in front of the headlights, and had been damn near guillotined. Their bodies were still warm.'

The second grunted, approached the window, studied its neat hole and said, 'The bunch that did this would be too sharp to leave a print.'

'They weren't too sharp to leave the rings,' Matthew pointed out.

'Now you've got an angle there,' conceded the other. 'We'll test for prints anyway.'

A taxi swung into the dark street and pulled up behind the police car. An elegantly dressed, fussy looking and agitated individual clambered out and rushed to the waiting group. Keys jangled in his well-manicured hand.

'Gregory, the manager. You phoned me,' he explained. 'Gentlemen, this is awful! That window display is worth a lot of money, a lot of money. What a loss!'

'How about letting us in?' asked one of the policemen, unmoved by this demonstration of grief.

'Of course, of course.'

Jerkily he opened the gate, unlocked the door, using six keys for the job. They walked inside. Gregory switched on the shop's lights, stuck his head between plate glass shelves and surveyed his depleted window.

'All those beautiful watches!' he groaned.

'It's terrible, it's terrible,' said one of the policemen, speaking with mock solemnity. He favoured his fellows with a wink.

Gregory leaned farther over, the better to inspect an empty corner. 'All gone,' he moaned. 'All my show of the finest makes in – *Yeeouw!*' His yelp made them jump. Gregory bucked as he tried to force himself through the shelves toward the grille and the window beyond it. 'My watch, my own watch!'

The others peered over his shoulders just in time to see the gold buckle of a black velvet fob go through the hole in the window. Matthew was the first outside, his flashlight searching the pavement. Then he saw the watch. It was moving rapidly along against the angle of the wall but it stopped dead as his beam settled upon it. He caught a brief glimpse of something else equally bright and metallic as it scooted swiftly into the darkness outside the circle of his light.

Picking up the watch, Matthew stood and listened. The noises of the others coming out prevented him from hearing clearly but he could have sworn he'd heard a tiny whirring noise and a quick, juicy ticking that was not coming from the instrument in his hand. Must have been his imagination. Frowning, he turned to the others.

'Nobody was here,' he asserted. 'Looks like it dropped out of his pocket and rolled.'

A silly suggestion, he thought. How could a watch roll that far, especially with a fob on it? What the devil was happening this night? Far up the street something screeched, made a strange bubbling noise and stopped. He shuddered. He could make a shrewd guess at the cause of that sound. He glanced questioningly at the others but they didn't seem to have heard.

The morning newspapers gave the matter some space. The total, they said, was sixty watches and eight cats, also various oddments from the stock of a local scientific instrument maker. The details were fairly lavish but not complete. The rest came later.

Burman was there when I arrived. He appeared uneasy and a little short-tempered. Over in one corner the coffin was ticking away steadily, its noise much louder than it had been the previous day. The thing sounded a veritable hive of industry.

'Well?' I invited.

'It has moved around a lot during the night,' said Burman. 'It has broken a couple of thermometers and taken the mercury from them. I found some drawers and cupboards shut, others wide open, but I've a suspicion that a search has been made through the lot. A packet of nickel foil has vanished and a coil of copper wire has gone with it. A small platinum crucible has disappeared.' He pointed an angry finger at the bottom of the door. 'And I blame it for gnawing ratholes in that. They weren't there yesterday.'

Sure enough there were a couple of holes in the bottom of the door. But no rat made them. They were neat and smooth and round, almost as if a carpenter had cut them with a keyhole saw.

'Where's the sense in it making those? It can't crawl through apertures that size.'

'Where's the sense in the whole affair?' countered Burman. He glowered at the machines which stared back at him with its expressionless lenses and continued to make mysterious noises. *Tick-tick-tick!* it said. Then, suddenly, *whirr-thump-click!*

This was followed by a thin and very high-pitched whine. Something small, metallic and glittering shot inward through one of the ratholes, fled across the floor to the machine. A trapdoor opened and swallowed it with such swiftness that it had gone before we'd had a chance to react. The thing had been a cylindrical, polished object resembling the shuttle of a sewing-machine but about four times the size. It had been dragging something smaller and also metallic.

With considerable emphasis, Burman voiced a strange word. He foraged around the laboratory, found a three-foot length of half-inch steel rod. Dragging a chair to the door, he seated himself, gripped the rod like a war-club and watched the ratholes. The machine watched him with bland indifference and went on ticking.

Ten minutes later there came a loud click and another high-pitched whine. Nothing darted inward through the holes, but the curious object we'd already seen – or another one exactly like it – dropped out of the trap and made a beeline for the door. Coming from the wrong direction, it caught Burman by surprise. He made a wild swipe with the rod as the thing sped past his feet and out through a hole. It had vanished even as his bludgeon hit the floor.

'Damn!' swore Burman, aggravated. He held the rod loosely in his grip while he glared at the industrious coffin. 'I'd smash it to bits except that I'd like to get one of these small gadgets first.'

'Look out!' I yelled.

He was too late. He ripped his attention away from the machine and turned it toward the holes, swinging up the heavy length of steel, a startled look on his face. But his reaction was far too slow. Three of the little mysteries were through the holes and halfway across the floor before his weapon was ready to descend. The coffin swallowed them with the crash of a trapdoor.

The invading trio had rushed through in single file, giving a better view of themselves this time. The first two were golden shuttles identical with the first one. The third was bigger, faster, even more agile. It had a gleaming blade projecting from its front, a thing like a surgeon's scalpel. The blade appeared to be tipped with red.

Next came an irritated scratching upon the outside of the door and a white-tipped paw poked tentatively through one of the holes. The cat backed away when Burman opened the door but looked with longing at the laboratory. Its presence needed no explaining; the hunt was on and it knew where the prey had gone. This was an ally worth having. Given the chance, it might make a catch.

We enticed it in with fair words and soothing noises. Its eagerness overcame its distrust of strangers and it entered. Burman closed the door behind it, an unwise move seeing that the quarry could get through the holes but the cat could not. Grasping his steel rod, Burman resumed his seat by the door, attempted to keep one eye on the holes and the other on the cat. He couldn't do both but he tried. The cat sniffed and prowled around and mewed defeatedly. It seemed to be seeking by sight rather than scent. There wasn't any scent characteristic of rodents.

With feline persistence the animal searched the whole laboratory. Several times it passed the humming, ticking coffin but showed no interest in it. In the end, the cat gave it up, sat on the corner of the table and started grooming itself.

Tick-tick-tick! went the machine. Then *whirr-thump!* A trap popped open, a shuttle shot out and raced for the door. A second one followed it. The first was too fast even for the cat, too fast for the surprised Burman as well. *Bang!* The steel rod clouted the floor as the leading shuttle bulleted triumphantly through a hole.

But the cat got the second one. With a mighty leap, paws extended, claws out, it caught its victim a foot from the door. It tried to pin down the polished, slippery thing, failed, lost it for a moment. The shuttle whisked around in a sharp loop. The cat got it again, lost it again, emitted an angry snarl and batted it against the skirting board. The shuttle lay there upside-down, four midget wheels in its underside spinning madly with a faint whine.

Eyes afire with excitement, Burman dropped his weapon and went to pick up the shuttle. At the same time the cat slunk toward it ready to play with it. The shuttle lay there, helplessly functioning upon its back, but before either could reach it the big machine across the room went *clunk!*, opened a trap and ejected another gadget.

The cat responded with the promptness of which only a cat is capable. It pounced upon the newcomer. Then followed pandemonium. The prey made an agile swerve and showed a fitful gleam of gold. The cat swerved with it, cursed and spat. Black and white fur whirled around in a fighting haze in which gold occasionally shone. The cat's hissings and spittings overlay a persistent whine that swelled and sank in the manner of accelerating or decelerating gears.

A gasp came from the cat. Blood spotted the floor. The animal clawed wildly, let out another gasp followed by a gurgle. It shivered and flopped, a stream of crimson pouring from a great gash in its gullet.

There was barely time to take in this ghastly scene before the victor made for Burman. He was standing by the skirting board with the still humming shuttle in his hand; it was obvious in the circumstances that his capture had some way of radiating a call for help. Burman's face

wore a look of horror but he retained enough presence of
mind to make a frantic jump a second before the oncoming
menace could reach his feet.

He landed behind the thing but it reversed in its own
length and came for him again. Its scalpel shone like a
mirror as it banked at tremendous speed and the shine was
blocked with crimson for the first two inches of the blade.
Burman jumped over it again, reached the laboratory table
and got on top of it.

By this time I'd snatched up the steel rod and tried to
whack the buzzing lump of wickedness through the window
and over the roofs. It was a waste of time. The thing
whirled this way and that, dodging the very tip of the
descending steel, and flashing twice around the table on
which Burman had taken refuge. Apart from avoiding my
blows the thing ignored me. It was responding wholly and
solely to appeals from the shuttle.

The rod made another desperate swipe and missed by
no more than a millimetre. Something whipped through
the holes in the door and raced to the big machine. There
was a snapping sound of a trap opening and closing while
all the time was that steady *tick-tick-tick!*

Unexpectedly, the mechanical assassin on the floor
ceased its gyrations around the table. With a hard click
and a different, louder *whirr!* it raced up one leg of the
table, doing it with all the assured ease of a hunting spider.
It reached the top.

Burman left his sanctuary with the frantic leap of a man
who has no desire to have the feet lopped from his legs.
His face was white but he was still clinging to the shuttle.

'The machine,' he shouted. 'We must bash it until it
stops.'

Thunk! went the coffin. A trap gaped and released another
demon with a scalpel. Tzz-z-z! a third one shot in through
a hole in the door. Four shuttles came behind it, made for

the machine, reached it safely. A fifth object entered more slowly. It was dragging an automobile valve-spring.

With another jump Burman cleared an attacker. A second sheared off the toe of his right shoe as he landed. Again he reached the table from which his first foe had departed. All three scalpel-bearers immediately made for the table with an eager vim that was frightening.

'Drop that damned shuttle!' I bawled.

He didn't drop it. As the fighting trio whirred up the tablelegs he flung the shuttle with all his might at the coffin that had given it birth. It struck, dented the casing, fell to the floor. It lay battered and noiseless, its small motive wheels stilled.

The armed contraptions mounting the table changed their purpose coincidentally with the shuttle's smashing. With one accord they dived to the floor, crossed it and bolted through the holes in the door. A fourth emerged from the machine, escorted two shuttles to the door and these three vanished beyond.

A few seconds later a new thing, different from all the rest, came in through a hole. It was long, round-bodied, snub-nosed, roughly the size of a policeman's baton, had six wheels underneath and a double row of serrations in front. It almost sauntered across the room while we watched fascinatedly. Its front serrations jerked and shifted when it climbed the lowered trap-lid and got into the machine. They were midget caterpillar tracks.

By now Burman had had more than enough. He made up his mind: experimentation had gone too far. It must be stopped. Finding the steel rod, he gripped it firmly and approached the coffin. Its lenses seemed to leer at him as he stood before it. Twelve years of intensive work about to be destroyed. Endless days and nights of concentrated effort to be undone in one minute. But Burman was past caring. With a ferocious swing he demolished a glass window, with a fierce thrust he shattered the assembly of wheels and cogs behind it.

The coffin shuddered and slid beneath his rain of violent blows. Trapdoors dropped open, spilled out inactive samples of the thing's metal brood. Grindings and raspings came from its insides as Burman battered it to pieces. Then at last it was silent, inert, a useless mass of twisted and broken parts.

'That,' said Burman, breathing heavily, 'is that!'

He opened the door to see if the noise had attracted any attention. It hadn't. There was a lifeless shuttle lying in the doorway, another a yard behind it. The first had a silver bracelet attached by a tiny hook at its rear. The nosecap of the second had spread open fanwise, like an iris diaphragm, and inside it a pair of jointed arms were hugging a medium-sized diamond. Obviously they were bringing home the loot when the end of the coffin called a general halt. Though inactive, they were quite undamaged. It was clear that in some way they had been controlled by the coffin and had drawn power from it. This meant that the problem had been solved. By destroying the one, Burman had destroyed the lot.

Burman got his breath back and started talking. 'The Robot Mother. That's what I made – a smaller, more compact model of the Robot Mother, an apparatus that can create other gadgets. I ought to have had the sense to see that I was constructing the most dangerous thing in existence, a thing that shares with human beings the ability to propagate. Thank God it's been stopped before it's had time to become a major menace.'

Remembering his claim to have got it from the extreme future, I said, 'So that's the eventual master, or mistress, of Planet Earth. A dismal prospect for posterity, isn't it?'

'Not necessarily. I don't know how far I got but I suspect it was such a tremendous distance into the future that the world had become sterile from humanity's viewpoint. Maybe people had emigrated to somewhere else in the cosmos, leaving their semi-intelligent machines to fight for existence or die. The machines fought – and survived.'

'And end up trying to alter the past in their favour.'

'No, I don't think so.' Burman was calmer by now. 'It was a risky but interesting experiment, in my opinion. It would decide once and for all whether theory accords with fact. Theory says you cannot go back and change the past without creating an impossible paradox in the present and the future. But that's human theory. Machines are empirical, they operate wholly on facts. Given an idea, all that matters is whether it works. Either it does or it doesn't and to hell with philosophical reasonings.'

'Well, this one didn't.'

'It couldn't,' said Burman, flatly. 'It was doomed in advance. There are no robots in the next few centuries. Hence, any intruders in the present time must have been wiped out and forgotten more thoroughly than Atlantis.'

'Along with all your own data,' I suggested.

'Yes,' he agreed. 'I now understand that the psych-ophone can never be of real use to me. It permits me to discover or invent only those things that history decrees I shall invent and which, therefore, I shall find with or without the contraption. I can't play tricks with history, past or future. So my data is useless. I'll scrap the lot and it will be no loss.'

It was difficult to find a flaw in his reasoning, so I didn't argue but merely remarked, 'There was something bee-like about this bunch. You built a hive containing a queen and from it came workers, warriors and one drone.'

'You're right and I'm going to be stuck with the cost of the nectar they brought in. Watches and jewellery and other expensive items. A pretty penny! Not to mention claims for dead cats.' He pulled a sour face, added in brighter tone, 'It's a comfort that it's been stopped before things became lots worse. All's well that ends well.'

He got a cockeyed amen to that. There sounded a whine of midget motors. A golden shuttle slid through one of the ratholes, sensed the death of the Robot Mother, whirled round in alarm and bolted out.

If Burman had been shaken before, he was doubly so now. He went to the door, stared incredulously at the exit just used by the shuttle, then at the other undamaged but lifeless shuttles lying in the room.

'Your bee analogy was perfect,' he growled. 'A young queen got loose. There's another swarm somewhere.'

Another swarm there was. For the next forty-eight hours it played merry hell. Burman spent a lot of time at police headquarters trying to convince them that his evidence was not just a fantastic story. His veracity was supported by the equally fantastic reports that came rolling in, by the hour.

To start with, old Gildersome heard a crash in his shop at midnight, thought of his valuable stock of cameras and movie projectors, pulled on his pants and rushed downstairs. A razor-sharp instrument stabbed him through the right instep when partway down and he fell the rest of the way. He lay there, bleeding and semi-stunned while things clicked, ticked and whirred in the darkness all around. One by one, the contents of his box of telescopic lenses went through a gap at the bottom of the door. A quantity of projector parts, mostly cogs and wheels, went with them.

Ten people complained of being robbed in the night of watches and clocks. Two were hysterical. One swore that the bandit had been 'a six-inch cockroach' which hummed like a toy dynamo. Jumping out of bed he'd put his foot on it and felt its cold hardness slip away from beneath him. Filled with revulsion, he had dived back into bed just as 'another cockroach' scuttled toward him. Burman didn't bother to tell this agitated complainant how near he had come to an amputation.

Thirty more reports came in next day. A score of houses had been entered and four shops robbed by ticking, buzzing things that had more agility and furtiveness than rats. One was seen racing along a lane by a night-homing railway worker. He tried to grab it, lost his right forefinger and thumb so slickly that he hardly felt the pain.

Rare metals and finely machined parts were the chief prey of these marauders. Like everything else in existence, they responded to their needs – and their needs were robotic. Burman made use of this fact by baiting them.

'The great majority of reports centre on this street,' he said. 'A stolen alarm clock was abandoned over there. Two automobiles were robbed of small parts nearby. A number of shuttles have been seen sneaking to or from this area. Five cats have been knocked off within a couple of hundred yards. Every other incident has taken place within easy reach.'

'Which means you think the queen bee is hiding in this vicinity?'

'That's the way it looks.' He gazed up and down the slumbering road over which a crescent moon shed a sickly light. It was two o'clock in the morning. 'With luck, we'll persuade them to give us a lead to the den.'

He attached one end of a reel of strong cotton to a silver chain, nailed the reel to the wall, dropped the chain on the pavement. Farther along he did the same with a broken watch. Then he distributed several small gear-wheels, some small bunches of copper wire and other attractive oddments, each linked to its own reel.

Four hours later we returned accompanied by police. They had sledge-hammers and crowbars with them. All of us were wearing steel leg-and-foot shields knocked up at short notice by a local sheet-metal worker.

The bait had been taken. A number of cotton strands had been broken after being unreeled a short distance, but others were intact. All of them either led to or pointed to a cellar below an abandoned and dilapidated warehouse. Looking down through the grating in the pavement we could see several telltale strands running through a gap in the rotting windowframe below.

Burman snapped, 'Right!' and we went at the warehouse's main door in a rush. Corroded locks broke open, rusty hinges collapsed, we poured into a rubbish-littered floor and raced down to the cellar.

There was a small, coffin-shaped thing standing against one wall, ticking steadily while its lenses stared at us with ghastly lack of emotion. It was very similar to the Robot Mother but only a quarter of the size, and it had the scrappy look of an apparatus thrown together in a hurry – but workable. In the light of a police torch it was a brooding, ominous thing exuding its full share of menace. Around it, an active clan darted over the floor, buzzing and clicking in metallic fury.

Amid angry whirrings and frequent squeals as attacking scalpels hit steel, we waded through the lot. Burman was first to reach the coffin. He struck it a fearful clout with a twelve-pound sledge-hammer then bashed it to ruin with a rapid and violent succession of blows. He finished exhausted. The daughter of the Robot Mother was no more, nor did her alien tribe move or stir.

Sitting himself on a rickety wooden crate, Burman mopped his forehead and said, 'That's the end of it, thank God!'

Tick-tick-tick!

He shot to his feet, a wild look in his eyes, and took a fresh grip on his hammer.

'Only my watch,' apologized one of the policemen. 'It's a cheap one and a bit noisy.' He took it out and showed it to the bothered Burman.

'*Tick! Tick!*' said the watch, with mechanical aplomb.

INTO YOUR TENT I'LL CREEP

Morfad sat in the midship cabin and gloomed at the wall. He was worried and couldn't conceal the fact. The present situation had all the frustrating qualities of a gigantic rat-trap. One could escape it only with the combined help of all the other rats.

But the others weren't likely to lift a finger either on his or their own behalf. He felt sure of that. How can you persuade people to try escape a dangerous predicament when you can't convince them that they're in one, right up to the neck?

A rat runs around a trap only because it is grimly aware of the trap's existence. So long as it remains blissfully ignorant of its captivity, it does nothing. On this very world a horde of highly intelligent aliens had done nothing about it through the whole of their history. Fifty sceptical Altairans weren't likely to step in and succeed where four thousand million Terrans had failed.

He was still sitting there and brooding when Haraka came in and informed, 'We leave at sunset.'

Morfad said nothing.

'I'll be sorry to go,' added Haraka. He was the ship's captain, a big, burly sample of Altairan life. Rubbing flexible fingers together, he went on, 'We've been lucky to discover this planet, exceedingly lucky. We've become blood-brothers of a life-form fully up to our own standards of intelligence, space-traversing like ourselves, friendly and co-operative.'

Morfad said nothing.

'Their reception of us has been most cordial,' Haraka continued enthusiastically. 'Our people will be greatly heartened when they hear our report. A great future lies before us, there's no doubt of that. A Terran-Altairan combine will be invincible. Between us we'll be able to explore and exploit the entire galaxy.'

Morfad said nothing.

Cooling down, Haraka frowned at him. 'What's the matter with you, Misery-face?'

'I am not overjoyed.'

'Anyone can see that much. You have the expression of a very sour *shamsid* on an aged and withered bush. And at a time of triumph, too! Are you ill?'

'No.' Turning slowly, Morfad looked him straight in the eyes. 'Do you believe in psionic faculties?'

Haraka reacted as if caught on one foot. 'Well, I don't know. I am a captain, a trained engineer-navigator and as such I cannot pretend to be an expert upon extraordinary abilities. You ask me something I am not qualified to answer. How about you? Do you believe in them?'

'I do – *now*.'

'Now? Why now?'

'The belief has been thrust upon me.' Morfad hesitated, went on with a touch of desperation. 'I have discovered that I am telepathic.

Surveying him with slight incredulity, Haraka said, 'You've discovered it? You mean it has come upon you recently?'

'Yes.'

'Since when?'

'Since we arrived on Terra.'

'I don't understand this at all,' confessed Haraka, baffled.

'Do you assert that some peculiarity on Terra's conditions has suddenly enabled you to read my thoughts?'

'No, I cannot read your thoughts.'

'But you've just said that you have become telepathic.'

'So I have. I can hear thoughts as clearly as if the words were being shouted aloud. But not your thoughts nor those of any member of our crew.'

Haraka leaned forward, his features intent. 'Ah, you have been hearing *Terran* thoughts, eh? And what you've heard has got you worried? Morfad, I am your captain, your commander. It is your bounden duty to tell me of anything suspicious about these Terrans.' He waited a bit, urged impatiently, 'Come on, speak up!'

'I know no more about these humanoids than you do,' said Morfad. 'I have every reason to believe them genuinely friendly but I don't know the nature of their thoughts.'

'But, by the stars, Morfad, you have asserted – '

'We are talking at cross-purposes,' Morfad interrupted. 'Whether I do or do not overhear Terran thoughts depends upon what one means by Terrans.'

'Look,' insisted Haraka, fed up with word-play, 'exactly whose thoughts *do* you hear?'

Steeling himself, Morfad said flatly, 'Those of Terran dogs.'

'Dogs?' Haraka lay back and stared at him. '*Dogs?* Are you serious?'

'I have never been more so. I can hear dogs and no others. Don't ask me why because I don't know. It is a freak of circumstance.'

'And you have listened to their minds ever since we arrived on this planet?'

'Yes.'

'What sort of things have you heard?'

'I have had pearls of alien wisdom cast before me,' declared Morfad, 'and the longer I consider them the more they scare hell out of me.'

'Get busy frightening me with a few samples,' invited Haraka, suppressing a smile.

'Quote: the supreme test of intelligence is the ability to live as one pleases without working,' recited Morfad. 'Quote: the art of retribution is that of concealing it beyond all suspicion. Quote: the sharpest, most subtle, most effective weapon in the cosmos is flattery.'

'Huh?'

'Quote: if a creature is capable of thought, it likes to think that it is God. Treat it as God and it becomes one's willing slave.'

'Oh, no!' denied Haraka.

'Oh, *yes!*' insisted Morfad. He waved a disdainful hand toward the nearest port. 'Out there are three or four thousand million petty gods. They are eagerly panted after, fawned upon, gazed at with worshipping eyes. Gods are very gracious toward those who love them.' He made a spitting sound that lent emphasis to what followed. 'The lovers know it – and love comes cheap.'

Haraka said uneasily, 'I think you're crazy.'

'Quote: to rule successfully the ruled must remain happily unconscious of it.' Again the spitting sound. 'Is that crazy? I don't think so. It makes sense. It works. It's working out there right now.'

'But – '

'Take a look at this.' He tossed a small object into Haraka's lap. 'What is it?'

'It's what they call a biscuit, a cracker.'

'Correct. To make it some Terrans ploughed fields in all kinds of weather, rain, wind and sunshine, sowed wheat, reaped it with the aid of machinery that other Terrans had sweated to built. They transported the wheat, stored it, milled it, enriched the flour by various processes, baked it, packaged it, shipped it all over the world. When humanoid Terrans want crackers they've got to put in many man-hours to get them.'

'So – ?'

'When a dog wants one he sits up, waves his forepaws and admires his god. That's all. Just that.'

'But, darn it, man, dogs are relatively stupid.'

'So it seems,' said Morfad, dryly.

'They can't really *do* anything effective.'

'That depends on what one regards as effective.'

'They haven't got fingers or hands.'

'And don't need them – having brains.'

'Now see here,' declaimed Haraka, openly irritated, 'we Altairans have invented and developed ships capable of roaming the spaces between the stars. The Terrans have done the same. Terran dogs have not done it and won't do it in the next million years. When one dog has the brains and ability to get to another planet I'll eat my cap.'

'You can start eating right now,' Morfad suggested. 'We have two dogs on board.'

Haraka let go a grunt of disdain. 'The Terrans have given us those as a memento.'

'Sure they gave them to us – at whose behest?'

'It was a wholly spontaneous gesture.'

'Was it?'

'Are you suggesting that dogs put the idea into their heads?' Haraka demanded.

'I know they did,' retorted Morfad, looking grim. 'And we've not been given two males or two females. Oh, not, not on your life. One male and one female. The givers said we could breed them. Thus in due course our own worlds can become illuminated with the undying love of man's best friend.'

'Nonsense!' said Haraka.

Morfad gave back, 'You're obsessed with the old, out-of-date idea that conquest must be preceded by aggression. Can't you understand that a wholly alien species just naturally uses wholly alien methods? Dogs employ their own tactics, not ours. It isn't within their nature or abilities to take us over with the aid of ships, guns and a great hullabaloo. It *is* within their nature and abilities to creep in upon us, their eyes shining with calculated hero-worship. If we don't watch out we'll be mastered by a horde of loving creepers.'

'I can invent a word for your mental condition,' said Haraka. 'You're suffering from caniphobia.'

'With good reasons.'

'Imaginary ones.'

'Yesterday I looked into a dogs' beauty shop. Who was doing the bathing, scenting, powdering and primping? Other dogs? Hah! Humanoid females were busy dolling them up. Was *that* imaginary?'

'You can call it a Terran eccentricity. It means nothing whatever. Besides, we've got some peculiar habits of our own.'

'You're dead right there,' agreed Morfad. 'And I know one of yours. So does the entire crew.'

Haraka narrowed his eyes. 'You might as well name it. I am not afraid to see myself as others see me.'

'All right. You've asked for it. You think a lot of Kashim. He always has your ear. You will listen to him when you will listen to nobody else. Everything he says is the essence of pure wisdom – to you.'

'So you're jealous of Kashim, eh?'

'Not in the least,' assured Morfad, making a disparaging gesture. 'I merely despise him for the same reason that everyone else holds him in contempt. He is a professional toady. He spends most of his time fawning upon you, flattering you, pandering to your ego. He is a natural-born creeper who gives you the Terradog treatment. You like it. You bask in it. It affects you like an irresistible drug. It works – and don't tell me that it doesn't because all of us know that it *does*.'

'I am not a fool. I have Kashim sized up. He does not influence me to anything like the extent you believe.'

'Three to four thousand million Terrans have four hundred million dogs sized up and are equally convinced that no dog has a say in anything worth a hoot.'

'I don't believe it.'

'Of course you don't. I had little hope that you would. Morfad is telling you these things and Morfad is either crazy or a liar. But if Kashim were to tell you while prostrated at the foot of your throne you would swallow his story hook, line and sinker. Kashim has a Terradog mind and uses Terradog logic, see?'

'My disbelief has better basis than that.'

'For instance?' Morfad invited.

'Some Terrans are telepathic. Therefore if this myth of subtle mastery by dogs were a fact, they'd know of it. Not a dog would be left alive on this world.' Haraka paused, finished pointedly, 'They don't know of it.'

'Terran telepaths hear the minds of their own kind but not those of dogs. I hear the minds of dogs but not those of any other kind. As said before, I don't know why this should be. I know only that it *is*.'

'It seems nonsensical to me.'

'It would. I suppose you can't be blamed for taking that viewpoint. My own position is difficult; I'm like the only person with ears in a world that is stone-deaf.'

Haraka thought it over and said after a while, 'Suppose I were to accept everything you've said at face value – what do you think I should do about it?'

'Refuse to take the dogs,' said Morfad promptly.

'That's more easily said than done. Good relations with the Terrans are of vital importance. How can I reject a warmhearted gift without offending the givers?'

'All right. Don't reject it. Modify it instead. Ask for two male or two female dogs. Make it plausible by quoting an Altairan law prohibiting the importation of alien animals that are capable of natural increase.'

'I can't do that. It's far too late. We've already accepted the animals and expressed our gratitude for them. What's more, their ability to breed is an essential part of the gift, the basic intention of the givers. They've presented us with a new species, an entire race of dogs.'

'You've said it!' confirmed Morfad.

'For the same reason we cannot very well prevent them from breeding when we get back home,' Haraka pointed out. 'From now on we and the Terrans are going to do quite a lot of visiting. Immediately they discover that our dogs have failed to multiply they'll become sentimental and generous and dump another dozen on us. Or maybe a hundred. We'll then be no better off than we were before.'

'All right, all right.' Morfad shrugged with weary resignation. 'If you're going to concoct a major objection to every possible solution we may as well surrender without a fight. Let's abandon ourselves to becoming another dog-dominated species. Requote: to rule successfully the ruled must be happily unconscious of it.' He gave Haraka the sour eye. 'If I had my way I'd wait until we were far out in free space and then give those two dogs the hearty heave-ho out of the nearest hatch.'

Haraka smirked in the manner of one about to demolish a cockeyed story once and for all. 'And if you did that it would be proof beyond all argument that you're afflicted with a delusion.'

Emitting a deep sigh, Morfad asked, 'Why would it?'

'You'd be slinging out two prime members of the master race. Some domination, eh?' Haraka grinned again. 'Listen, Morfad, according to your own story you know something never before known or suspected and you're the only one today who does know it. That should make you a mighty menace to the entire species of dogs. They wouldn't let you live long enough to thwart them or even to go round advertising the truth. You'd soon be deader than a low-strata fossil.' He walked to the door, held it open while he made his parting shot. 'You look healthy enough to me.'

Morfad shouted at the closing door, 'Doesn't follow that because I can hear their thoughts they must necessarily hear mine. I doubt that they can because it's just a freakish – '

The door clicked shut. He scowled at it, walked twenty times up and down the cabin, finally resumed his chair and sat in silence while he beat his brains around in search of a satisfactory solution.

'The sharpest, most subtle, most effective weapon in the cosmos is flattery.'

Yes, he was seeking a means of coping with four-footed warriors incredibly skilled in the use of Creation's sharpest weapon. Professional fawners, creepers, worshippers, man-lovers, ego-boosters, trained to near-perfection through countless generations in an art against which there seemed to be no effective defence.

How to beat off the coming attack? How to contain it, counter it?

'Yes, God!'

'Certainly, God!'

'Anything you say, God!'

How to protect oneself against this insidious technique, how to quarantine it or –

By the stars! that was it! *Quarantine* them! On Pladamine, the useless world, the planet nobody wanted. They could breed there to their limits and meanwhile cajole and dominate the herbs and bugs. And a soothing reply would be ready for any nosey Terran tourist.

'The dogs? Oh, sure, we've still got them, lots of them. They're doing fine. Got a nice world of their very own. Place called Pladamine. If you wish to go see them, it can be arranged.'

A wonderful idea. It would solve the problem while creating no hard feelings among the Terrans. It would prove useful in the future and to the end of time. Once dumped on Pladamine no dog could ever escape by its own efforts. Any tourists from Terra who insisted on bringing dogs along could be persuaded to leave them in the canine heaven specially created by Altair. There the dogs would find themselves unable to boss anything higher than other dogs. They could be parasites on each other and if they didn't like it they could lump it.

No use putting this scheme to Haraka who obviously was prejudiced. He, Morfad, would save it for the authorities back home. Even if they found it difficult to credit his story they'd still take the necessary action on the principle that it is better to be sure than sorry. Yes, they'd play safe and give Pladamine to the dogs.

Standing on a cabin seat, he gazed out and down through the observation-port. Far below, a great mob of Terrans waited to witness the coming take-off and cheer them on their way. He noticed beyond the back of the crowd a small, absurdly-groomed dog dragging a Terran female at the end of a thin, light chain. Poor girl, he thought. The dog leads, she follows yet believes *she* is taking *it* someplace.

Finding his stereo camera, he checked its controls, walked along the corridor and into the open airlock. It would be nice to have a souvenir picture of the big send-off audience. Reaching the rim of the lock, camera in hand, he tripped headlong over something four-legged and stubby-tailed that suddenly intruded itself between his feet. He dived outward, the camera still firmly in his grip, and went down fast through a whistling wind while shrill feminine screams came from among the watching crowd.

Haraka said, 'The funeral has delayed us two days. We'll have to make up the time as best we can.' He brooded a moment, added, 'I am very sorry about Morfad. He had a brilliant mind but it was becoming erratic toward the end. Oh, well, it's a comfort that the expedition has suffered only one fatality.'

'It could have been worse, sir,' responded Kashim. 'It could have been you. Praise the heavens that it was not.'

'Yes, it could have been me.' Haraka regarded him curiously. 'And would it have grieved you, Kashim?'

'Very much indeed, sir. I don't think anyone aboard

would feel the loss more deeply. My respect and admiration are such that – '

He ceased as something padded softly into the cabin, laid its head in Haraka's lap and gazed soulfully up at the captain. Kashim frowned with annoyance.

'Good boy!' approved Haraka, scratching the new-comer's ears.

'My respect and admiration,' repeated Kashim in louder tones, 'are such that – '

'Good boy!' said Haraka again. He gently pulled one ear, then the other, observed with pleasure the vibrating tail.

'As I was saying, sir, my respect – '

'Good boy!' Deaf to all else, Haraka slid a hand down from the ears and massaged under the jaw.

Kashim favoured Good Boy with a glare of concentrated hate. The dog rolled a brown eye sideways and looked at him without expression. From that moment Kashim's fate was sealed.

NOTHING NEW

The ship fled through sparkling darkness. There were orbs of flame and whorls of light and glittering spirals that told of multimillion suns and hidden planets stretching onward, ever onward through infinity. And through these streaked the ship, a superfast mote less in the vastness than a bulleting speck of dust, a speck that none the less bore its full quota of life.

At such pace went the vessel that nearer stars in its line of flight appeared gradually to drift apart hour by hour rather than month by month or year by year. It was a mote with a new power undreamed-of in long bygone days when one dead satellite had been claimed with a triumphant shout. A mote whose years were less than days and whose space-reach was enormously extended.

The man in its nose was not amazed by the near-invisible phenomenon of star-drift. It was a normal feature of his day and age, an accepted marvel often depicted on the telereceivers of stodgy stay-at-homes.

Olaf Redfern, the pilot, sat at his controls and gazed into the shining heavens with the calm, phlegmatic air of one to whom is given the task of finding very small pinheads in very large haystacks. With the aid of charts, instruments, computers the size of cigarette packs, plus the abilities of Navigator Paul Gildea and the luck of a Terran garnet in his finger ring, he had done it fifty times in the past and was confident of doing it a hundred times in the future.

Readjusting the controls which were complicated enough to make a major chore of creating a minor shift in flight-angle, he locked them on the fractionally altered course, remained staring steadily into expanding space. In short time Simkin, the official archaeologist, joined him, took the adjacent seat and studied the view.

'Someone once said,' he remarked, 'that it is better to travel than to arrive. I don't agree. One can become tired of living just in front of a low-pitched whistle while a multitude of candles float around in the night.'

'That's because you've little to do before we get there,' Redfern offered. 'Try piloting for a change. It'll keep you on your toes.'

'I'm too old to start afresh, too settled in my chosen field.' He threw Redfern a knowing smile. 'The thrill you get out of finding and landing on a strange world is no greater than the kick I get out of digging up an ancient artifact whole and unscratched.'

'Frankly, I don't see the fascination of your job,' said Redfern. 'It's rooted in the far past which is finished and done and gone for ever, whereas mine probes the future into which we're moving every minute. The future is controllable within limits. You can't do a darned thing about the past.'

'I agree. But still we have our surprises and our triumphs. After all, it was a bunch of hole-diggers who proved that highly intelligent life once existed on those twin worlds near Arcturus.'

'They're still dead worlds to me,' Redfern commented.

'Maybe so. The hole-diggers are carrying on, all the same. They're digging deeper. They want to know why life departed. Did it merely die out and, if so, of what cause? Or did it go elsewhere and, if so, by what means and whence? Answers to those questions may tell us things well worth knowing. We're never too big to learn.'

'Well, there's that about it,' Redfern conceded.

Falderson, the mass-sociologist, lumbered into the control-room and flopped on a seat. He was a big, paunchy man with a nervous twitch in his left eyebrow. The said twitch often served to fascinate alien life-forms while under cross-examination.

'We should land in about fourteen hours' time, according to Gildea's latest estimate,' he announced. 'And I hope to God they won't prove to be a gang of howling barbarians who'll throw things at us on sight. I hate to admit it but this long incarceration has loaded me with too much fat for primitive battles.'

'You'll lose the grease,' promised Redfern. 'It'll all boil out on the cooking-pot.'

'I can't imagine immortals being unlettered savages,' Simkin opined.

'Immortals?' Redfern eyed him incredulously. 'What are you talking about?'

Simkin registered equal surprise. 'Didn't you know that the planet we're seeking is rumoured to be populated by immortals?'

'First I've heard of it. I get flight instructions, the same as Gildea. We lug loads of experts hither and yon, seldom know or ask the reason why.' He frowned to himself, added, 'I just can't believe that anyone has discovered the secret of eternal life. I take that idea with a heavy cargo of salt.'

'So do we,' Simkin gave back. 'But legends often prove to be grossly distorted versions of original truths. Our present purpose is to determine the degree of distortion by discovering how much truth existed in the first place and, with luck, how much still exists.'

'Where do legends come into this?'

'You tell him – it's your pet subject,' Simkin suggested to Falderson.

NOTHING NEW 109

The mass-sociologist said, 'You've heard of the Alpedes, that seven-planet group beyond Rigel?'

'I ought to. I've been there twice. Come to that, we're not so far from them right now.'

'Then you'll know that all are populated by intelligent life-forms more or less civilized but not sufficiently advanced to be capable of constructing even an antiquated rocket-ship. Therefore it was quite impossible for them to have any contact with each other until Terrans arrived a couple of centuries ago and set up a small inter-system mail service.'

'Yes, a friend of mine is piloting for that outfit.'

'Well,' continued Falderson heavily, 'what with political, strategical, and commercial considerations coming first – not to mention the strong pull of other urgent interests in various other directions – it was quite a time before anyone got down to serious study of the sevenfold Alpedian cultural mores. A certain Professor Wade eventually buried himself in that task and after a couple of years he came up with a hair-raiser.'

'I view that as an understatement,' put in Simkin.

Taking no notice, Falderson continued, 'All seven planets had recorded histories available for study. And before the histories, all seven had the usual mass of legends. Naturally, since the planets lacked contact, their histories and legends had nothing in common other than minor items explainable by fortuitous circumstance. But there was one most remark-able exception: all seven planets nursed a fairy tale about a world of immortals.'

'But that suggests contact of some kind,' Redfern objected.

'Precisely! Yet their histories make no mention of it. The major event of their times left unrecorded. The height of their achievement ignored and allowed to be forgotten. Why? There has to be a reason.'

'What's your guess?'

'Current theory is that if ever contact was made it was

by proxy, it was done by others exactly as it is done today. And it was done in the far, far past before their history began to be written, in the misty days when legends were born. The logical supposition is that all seven planets were once visited by these immortals. All that is remembered of them today is their most striking attribute, immortality.'

'H'm!' mused Redfern. 'Twice can be coincidence. Three times can be coincidence. But the same story seven times over is odd to say the least. It needs explaining.'

'That's what Professor Wade thought. He dug deep into seven mythologies, came up with a couple more curious items. Firstly, the immortals had never visited the Alpedes themselves. That plays hob with our logical guess and the only alternative we can think up is that the story originated with some third party, some other visitors from space who picked it up and passed it on. Secondly, all seven legends agreed that the immortals lived on a very big world which was the only planet of a blue sun.'

'So – ?'

'So Wade beamed his findings back to Terra without delay. The cosmographologists and other eggheads were at once interested, seeing that several times clues of this sort have led us straight to other discoveries.'

'Thanks in part to archaeology,' Simkin put in, nudging the listener.

'The Rigel sector is only a quarter explored to date,' Falderson went on . 'All the same, we've got some good spectra charts of that locality. Analysis of them has revealed a definite blue-type sun not a long way from the Alpedes group. Astro-physicists agree that it's by far the likeliest primary in that area and they've calculated that it could have one large planet of rather low mass.'

'And that's where we're making for right now?' said Redfern.

'Yes, my boy.' Falderson stood up and patted his paunch. 'If we're lucky enough to lay our hands on the secret of life eternal, you may be roaming the spaceways for ever and ever, amen. As for me, I shall have to do something about this belly before it pins me flat on my face.'

He departed, leaving them to their thoughts while the ship sped onward and the starfield widened. After a bit, Simkin spoke.

'Do you now see the fascination of probing the past?'

'It has some interest for the snoopy type of mind,' Redfern admitted.

'There's plenty to be snooped for,' Simkin retorted. 'And that holds good for any one world, without ever seeing another. Take Terra, for example. We know more about our own planet than any in Creation. That's to be expected, isn't it? Yet there's an appalling amount we don't know and, perhaps, never will now.'

'Such as?'

'Terra's most widespread and well-established legend is that of the Great Flood. There's little doubt that it has real basis. Sometime in the remote past something of catastrophic proportions happened to Terra. It was a major disaster that knocked the human race an unknown distance down the ladder. The big number one question is: from what height did we fall?'

'We couldn't have dropped far,' Redfern opined. 'Before the Flood we were scratching in trees.'

'If we ever scratched in trees, which is highly debatable, it was umpteen millenia before the Flood. In between there was plenty of time for the human race to climb to the top and be knocked down a dozen times over. Look how far we've climbed in our present recorded history which covers less than ten thousand years. So where had we got and what were we doing and where were we going when the oceans piled up and roared over the land and brought us to near-extinction?'

'Don't ask me,' said Redfern. 'I wasn't there at the time.'

'Olaf, we could have been zooming around a lot longer

than we think,' offered Simkin, seriously. 'And for that reason I'd give my right hand to achieve the impossible.'

'Meaning what?'

'I'd give it for a good long look at whatever may be lying whole and undamaged beneath hundreds of fathoms of salt water and enormous layers of ooze. I'd give it to see what, if anything, was in existence before the valleys were raised and the hills made low, before small, hungry, bewildered bands of semi-savage survivors roamed the water-bedecked land.'

'Well,' commented Redfern, grinning, 'it would be nice to see your face if you dug out of the slime a spaceship twice as good as this one.'

'And it would be equally nice to see yours,' answered Simkin, 'when confronted with the evidence that we haven't yet regained the heights from which we fell.'

Redfern let that pass without argument. He was a pilot, eminently a practical man trained to cope with immediate problems and not much given to long-term speculation.

The astrophysicists proved one hundred per cent correct. The blue sun had one large planet of relatively low mass. It was not gaseous, it was not liquid. Thick vegetation covered its surface of loamy earth in which lurked sparse deposits of light metals, none whatever of heavy ones.

Everything suited a prompt landing. Tests proved the primary's radiations to be innocuous so far as humankind was concerned. The planet's atmosphere was on the thin side but had adequate oxygen content. Finally, the world most obviously was inhabited.

One low-altitude circumnavigation revealed much about its dominant life-form before a specimen had been encountered. Intelligence and vegetarianism were outstanding characteristics of the planetary scene. Sprawling towns of size and substance showed the former; great cultivated areas devoid of animal herds evidenced the latter.

Lying awkwardly in the nose and peering down through

the forward port, Falderson said after a while, 'Wholly agrarian. Note the lack of heavy industry. And the cities are small from the population viewpoint. They look big merely because of their lavish spread. Every house has a two-acre garden or bigger.'

'Fat lot of traffic either,' remarked Gildea. 'No railroads, no planes, no crowded motorways.'

'Even if you have the brains to design locomotives, planes and automobiles, you can't do a thing about them if there's a complete lack of natural resources,' said Redfern. 'It's a safe bet that this crowd has never boosted into space and never will. They're earthbound because they're without the facilities to get off the planet. Hm-m-m! It's going to be mighty interesting to see how many social problems have been created by sheer lack of what most inhabitable planets possess.'

'Take her down, Olaf,' ordered Gildea, pointing. 'Dump her by that city alongside the river. The place looks as important as any we've seen.'

'I'll go wake Taylor,' said Simkin, hurrying out.

Entering the mid-cabin he roused the linguist from his drug-induced slumbers. Taylor, a chronic sufferer from space migraine, emerged from unconsciousness, sat up, felt himself and blinked blearily.

'Mean to say we're there already?'

'We are. Your time-sense is distorted by sleep. Get busy sharpening your wits because you'll have to pick up new words, gestures, smoke-signals or whatever mighty fast.'

'I'll cope. That's my job, isn't it?' Taylor yawned, stretched his arms, relaxed again and sighed deeply. 'Let's hope this isn't another world like Comina. On that place it took me eight weeks to pick up their jaw-cracking speech and then I still limped at it. One soft, wet tongue can't reproduce the rhythmic smacking of horn-tipped palps.'

He reeled sidewise on his bunk as the room tilted. Simkin staggered, snatched at a handgrip on the wall and hung on. They stayed that way until the ship came level again and slowed with grinding noises along its belly-skids. It stopped.

'Thank the Lord,' said Taylor, fervently. 'Solid earth at last.'

'Since you love solidity so much,' Simkin remarked, 'Why do you choose sick-making trips in space?'

'Choose? That's a laugh! They said they wanted a volunteer and pointed straight at me.'

Leaving him, Simkin hastened to the nose. Falderson, Gildea and Redfern were there staring silently through the foreport. An approaching native was the object of their united attention.

The oncomer had emerged from the nearest house which was long, low and built of ornamentally carved stone blocks. He was making along his garden path towards the ship. His thoroughly alien appearance was nothing startling to space-sophisticated eyes long accustomed to forms more bizarre. The really surprising thing about him was his manner.

He made straight for the ship without awe, alarm, excitement, curiosity or any other visible symptom usually evident at first meetings on newfound worlds. On the contrary, he had no more than the stolidly helpful air of a rural farmer about to see whether a stalled motorist needed a hauling out of a mudhole.

If assistance was in his mind it was going to be a long time acoming because the best pace he could muster was no better than a crawl. He was a biped a little less than average manheight but wide and bulky. Two brilliant yellow eyes shone deep amid the lavish wrinkles covering his grey-skinned face. He wore neat clothing from which protruded a pair of columnar, flexible legs as grey and wrinkled as his face. The legs terminated in feet-pads resembling those of an elephant.

'Superficially humanoid,' decided Falderson. 'Notice his hands, just like mine only longer and narrower. I'll bet that basically he's reptilian; a lizard type that has learned to walk on its hind legs and battle the environment with its brains and forepaws.'

'He hasn't got a tail,' Redfern objected.

'Neither have you – today,' Gildea pointed out.

'He makes me think of someone I read about once,' mused Simkin. He racked his brains for the memory, found it. 'An ancient character named Chief Taumoto or something similar. He was revered in the Tonga Islands for more than two centuries. Science took a great interest in him because he was Terra's oldest living creature.'

'How old?' asked Redfern.

'Nobody knew for certain. All that could be said was that he was two-hundred plus when he died. He was a giant turtle holding a chieftain's rank.'

'This fellow has a turtle's neck, if ever I saw one,' commented Redfern, continuing to watch the visitor's laborious progress. 'And the mad velocity to go with it.'

'Where's Taylor?' demanded Falderson. 'Open the trap and drop the ladder, Olaf. If we don't go to meet this character we'll sit here for most of a month before he arrives.'

Scrambling down the metal rungs, they made toward the native. Seeing this, he promptly conserved energy by halting and waiting for them. Close up he looked decidedly less humanlike. The two parties stood and examined each other, the Terrans' attitude being one of frank and friendly interest while the grey-skinned one showed no more than patient submission to it.

Pointing to his own mouth, Taylor voiced a few random words with careful pronunciation and on a rising note of enquiry. The other responded with three or four liquid syllables spoken in little more than a whisper.

'They communicate vocally,' said Taylor, with much satisfaction. 'I'm sure I can pick up their speech without rupturing my epiglottis. Give me a few days and I'll have enough of the local lingo to get us by.'

Listening to this without any change of expression, the native waited until he had finished, then made a sluggish gesture toward the house and spoke invitingly.

'Varm!'

'Word number one,' Taylor remarked. 'Varm – come!'

They went. The going was the most difficult task with which they'd had to cope in years. The stupendous problem of how to annihilate vast distances by some means even faster than light now seemed less than that of how to walk at a steady pace of half a mile per hour.

With the other in the lead they crept in funereal procession around the end of the house, stopped before a pair of wooden doors hand-carved from top to bottom. Opening these, Greyface revealed a machine lurking within.

Taylor exclaimed, 'Seeing is believing – therefore I believe.'

The contraption was a light framework of aluminium tubes mounted on four canvas-tyred wheels and propelled by six sets of pedals. Three pairs of seats topped the assembly and provided accommodation for the source of motive power.

Drawing the multicycle out of its garage, they got it onto a narrow road which had the smooth hardness of frosted glass. Greyface mounted to the front right-hand seat, put an expert hand on the steering wheel. With the other hand he signed the Terrans to climb aboard.

'You're a qualified pilot, you take the other front seat,' Gildea suggested to Redfern.

Settling themselves in the seats, they put feet on pedals which were shaped like small plates and located a few inches too high.

The multicycle took off, gathered speed and shot along the road at a splended twelve miles per hour while a dozen legs pumped in perfect rhythm. Reaching a small crossroad, the captain of the crew jerked a thin cord fastened to his steering wheel and something in a box at the back let go with a shrill 'Wee-e-eek! Wee-e-eek!'

An answering 'Wee-e-eek!' came from a sideroad where a similar machine, with a crew of two, paused for them to pass. The two showed no surprise whatever at the sight of pedal-pushing Terrans.

Falderson, puffing and blowing in a rear seat beside Simkin, said, 'This'll reduce the waistline.'

'I'm baffled,' confessed Simkin, gazing around. 'Look at those richly decorated houses and well-tended gardens. Every home a picture. You'd think people capable of building to a top-grade standard could do better for themselves in the matter of transport.'

'With what?' Falderson asked. 'They can't make pies without pastry. They can't build cars without steel or run them without gasoline. By the looks of it, they don't have electric power either.' He breathed heavily as he pumped at his pedals. 'They ought to be a thoroughly frustrated species.'

'Why?'

'They're no more immortal than Mrs Murphy's dog – but the myth of immortality was born of something. Possibly they are exceptionally long-lived. If so, they've plenty of time on their hands as is suggested by the way they've dolled up everything in sight. That in turn means they've had time in which to accumulate wisdom much of which cannot be applied. Maybe they've invented half the things we've thought up, including means of conquering space, but in blueprint form only. That's as far as they can go. Concocters of dreams that never come true.'

'I'd like to stay here a year or two and dig into their past,' said Simkin.

'If there's another ten miles to go,' informed Falderson, 'I'll be staying here for keeps by reason of having dropped dead.'

At that point the machine turned to the right, trundled across a great square in which half a dozen fountains sent feathery sprays skyward. Braking to a stop before the ornate doors of a large, important building, Greyface dismounted. He entered the room, leaving them to examine the intricate murals on the corridor walls.

Elder Citizen Karfin attended to the papers on his desk with the slow, meticulous care of the aged. He was feeling the immense weight of a lifetime that now approximated eighteen thousand Earth-years. He had outlived the average Terran by more than two hundred times, he had outlived the rise and fall of Terran civilizations, he had outlived the whole of Terran recorded history. And this was not exceptional for his world, for his species. It was normal.

But now he knew he was becoming a little feeble and had no more than another three or four centuries to go. He looked up as somebody opened the door and came in. His old yellow eyes remained fixed upon the newcomer, steady and unwinking like those of a basking lizard.

In due time the visitor arrested his crawl and said in a respectful whisper, 'Honoured Elder, I am named Balaine.'

'Yes, Balaine, what is it that you wish?'

'Honoured Elder, at a little past the ninth hour a skyship of the pink-faced bipeds landed beyond my garden. There were five therein. I have brought them here knowing that you would wish to meet them.'

Karfin sighed and said, 'They came in my extreme youth. If I remember aright, they stayed for several orbits and told us of many wonders of the skies. When they did not come again I thought perhaps they had decided we were beneath their notice.' He sighed again. 'Oh, well, it cannot be said that they pester us. Please show them in.'

'Very well, Honoured Elder,' Balaine crept slowly away and brought them back.

The five Terrans lined up before him and eyed him with the bold, far-ranging adventurousness of their kind.

And not one of them knew that this was the second time.

EXPOSURE

The Rigelian ship came surreptitiously, in the deep of the night. Choosing a heavily forested area, it burned down a ring of trees, settled in the ash, sent out a powerful spray of liquid to kill the fires still creeping outward through the undergrowth.

Thin coils of smoke ascended from dying flames. Now adequately concealed from all directions but immediately above, the ship squatted amid towering conifers while its tubes cooled and contracted with metallic squeaks. There were strong smells of wood smoke, pine resin, acrid flame-killer and superheated metal.

Within the vessel there was a conference of aliens. They had two eyes apiece. That was their only positive feature: two eyes. Otherwise they had the formlessness, the almost liquid sloppiness of the completely malleable. When the three in the Chartroom consulted a planetary photograph they gestured with anything movable, a tentacle, pseudopod, a long, stump-ended arm, a mere digit, anything that struck their fancy at any given moment.

Just now all three were globular, shuffled around on wide, flat feet and were coated with a fine, smooth fur resembling green velvet. This similarity was due to politeness rather than desire. During conversation it was conventional to assume the shape and form of one's superior and, if he changed, to change with him.

So two were spherical and furry solely because Captain Id-Wan saw fit to be spherical and furry. Sometimes Id-Wan chose to be awkward. He'd give himself time to do a difficult shape, such as that of a reticulated molebater, then watch them straining their insides in effort to catch up.

Id-Wan said, 'We've recorded this world far out on its light side and not a spaceship near to challenge our presence. Evidently they have no spaceships.' He sniffed expressively and went on, 'These blown-up pictures are plenty good enough for our purpose. We've got the lay of the land and that's as much as we need.'

'There appears to be a lot of sea,' remarked Chief Navigator Bi-Nak, peering at a picture. 'Too much sea. More than half of it is sea.'

'Are you again belittling my conquests?' demanded Id-Wan, producing a striped tail.

'Not at all, captain,' assured Bi-Nak, dutifully imitating the tail. 'I was simply pointing out – '

'You point too much,' snapped Id-Wan. He turned to the third Rigelian. 'Doesn't he, Po-Duk?'

Pilot Po-Duk played safe by remarking, 'There are times and there are times.'

'That is truly profound,' commented Id-Wan, who had a robust contempt for neutrals. 'One points while the other functions as a fount of wisdom. It would be a pleasant change if for once you did the pointing and let Bi-Nak be the oracle. I could stand that. It would make for variety.

'Yes, captain,' agreed Po-Duk.

'Certainly, captain,' endorsed Bi-Nak.

'All right.' Irritably, Id-Wan turned back to the photographs. 'There are many cities. That means intelligent life. But we've seen no spaceships and we know that they're not established even on their own satellite. Hence, their intelligence is not of a high order.' He forced out a pair of mock hands so that he could rub them together. 'In other words, just the sort of creatures we want – ripe for the plucking.'

'You said that on the last planet,' informed Bi-Nak, whose strong point was not tact.

Id-Wan pulled in his tail and bawled, 'That was relative to worlds previouly visited. Up to that point they were the best. These are better.'

'We haven't seen them yet.'

'We shall. They will give us no trouble.' Id-Wan cooled down and mused aloud. 'Nothing gives us trouble and I doubt whether anything is capable of it. We have fooled half a hundred successive life-forms, all utterly different from any known in our home system. I anticipate no difficulties with another. Sometimes I think we must be unique in Creation. On every world we've explored the creatures were fixed in form, unchangeable. It would appear that we alone are not the slaves of rigidity.'

'Fixedness of form has its advantages,' denied Bi-Nak, a glutton for punishment. 'When my mother first met my father in the mating-field she thought he was a long-horned nodus and – '

'There you go again,' shouted Id-Wan, 'criticizing the self-evident.'

'I merely mentioned that my mother – '

'Dung to your mother,' said Id-Wan. He resumed with the photographs, indicating an area in the north of a great landmass. 'We are located there, well off the beaten tracks, yet within easy flying distance of four medium-sized towns. The really big cities which hold potential dangers are a good way off. Nearer villages are too small to be worth investigating. The medium-sized places are best for our purpose and, as I've said, there are four within reach.'

'Which we'll proceed to inspect?' suggested Po-Duk, mostly to show that he was paying attention.

'Of course. The usual tactics – two scouts each. One day's mixing among the natives and they'll get us all we need to know while the natives themselves learn nothing. After that – '

'A demonstration of power?' invited Po-Duk, eager to display some brilliance.

'Most certainly.' Id-Wan extended something like a hair-thin tentacle, used it to mark one of the four near towns. 'That place is as good as any. We'll scrape it clean off the planet's surface, then sit in space and see what they do about it. A major blow is the most effective way of persuading a world to reveal how highly it is organized.'

'If the last six planets are anything to go by,' ventured Po-Duk, 'we won't see much organization here. They'll panic or pray or both.'

'Much as we did when the Great Spot flared in the year of – ' began Bi-Nak. His voice trailed off as he detected a nasty gleam in Id-Wan's eyes.

Id-Wan turned to Po-Duk. 'Summon the chief of the scouts and tell him to hurry. I want action.' Staring hard at Bi-Nak he added, 'Action – not useless talk.'

The fat man whose name was Ollie Kampenfeldt waddled slowly through the dark toward the log hut whence came the thrum of a guitar and the sound of many voices. He was frowning as he progressed and mopping his forehead at regular intervals.

There were other log huts scattered around in the vicinity, a few showing lights but most in darkness. A yellow moon hung only a little above the big stockade of logs which ran right around the encampment; it stretched the shadows of the huts across neatly trimmed lawns and flowery borders.

Kampenfeldt lumbered into the noisy hut and yelped in shrill tones. The guitar ceased its twanging. The talking stopped. Presently the lights went out. He emerged accompanied by a small group of men most of whom dispersed.

Two stayed with him as he made toward the building

nearest the only gate in the heavy stockade. One of them was expostulating mildly.

'All right. So people need sleep. How were we to know it was that late? Why don'tcha put a clock in the place?'

'The last one got pinched. It cost me fifty.'

'Hah!' said the grumbler. 'So time doesn't matter. What do I care about it? There's plenty of it and I'm going no place. Make less noise and go to bed. We've got no clock because the joint is full of thieves. You'd think I was back in the jug.'

His companion on the other side of Kampenfeldt perked up with sudden interest. 'Hey, I didn't know you'd been in the clink.'

'After ten years on the night beat for a big paper you've been everywhere,' said the first. 'Even in a crackpotorium – even in a cemetery, for that matter.' Then he stopped his forward pacing, raised himself on tiptoe, stared northward. 'What was *that*?'

'What was what?' asked Kampenfeldt, mopping his brow and breathing heavily.

'Sort of ring of brilliant red light. It floated down into the forest.'

'Meteor,' suggested Kampenfeldt, little interested.

'Imagination,' said a third, having seen nothing.

'Too slow for a meteor,' declared the observer, still peering at the distant darkness. 'It floated down, like I said. Meteors don't float. They swoop, dive or plunge. Besides, I've never heard of one that shape or colour. More like a plane in flames. Maybe it was a plane in flames.'

'We'll know in an hour or so,' promised Kampenfeldt, disgruntled at the thought of further night-time disturbances.

'How'll we know?'

'The forest will be ablaze on a ten-mile front. It's drier than I've ever known it and ripe for the kindling.' He made a clumsy gesture with a fat hand. 'No fire, no plane.'

'Well, what else might it be?'

Kampenfeldt said wearily, 'I neither know nor care. I have to get up in the morning.'

He waddled into his hut, yawning widely. The others stood outside a short time and gazed northward. Nothing out of the ordinary was visible.

'Imagination,' repeated one.

'I saw something queer. Dunno what could be out there in all that lumber, but I saw something – and I've got good eyes.' He withdrew his attention, shrugged. 'Anyway, the heck with it.'

They went to bed.

Captain Id-Wan gave his orders to the chief of the scouts. 'Bring in some local life-forms. The nearest and handiest will do providing they're assorted, small and large. We want to test them.'

'Yes, captain.'

'Collect them only from the immediate neighbourhood. There is a camp to the south which undoubtedly contains superior forms. Keep away from it. Orders concerning that camp will be given to you after the more primitive forms have been tested.'

'I see, captain.'

'You do not see,' reproved Id-Wan. 'Otherwise you would have noted that I have created flexible digits upon my feet.'

'I beg your pardon, captain,' said the chief, hastening to fix himself up with similar extensions.

'The discourtesy is overlooked but do not repeat it. Send in the head radio technician, then get on with your task.'

To the radio officer, who made toes with praiseworthy promptitude, he said, 'What have you to report?'

'The same as we noted upon the approach – they fill the air.'

'What?' Id-Wan pulled surprisedly at an ear which he had not possessed a moment before. The ear stretched like soft rubber. 'I was not informed at the time.'

'I regret, I forgot to – ' commenced Bi-Nak, then ceased and strained himself before Id-Wan's eyes could catch him without a rubber ear.

'They fill the air,' repeated the radio technician, also dutifully one-eared. 'We've picked up their noises from one extreme to the other. There seems to be at least ten different speech patterns.

'No common language,' Bi-Nak mourned. 'That will complicate matters.'

'It will simplify matters,' Id-Wan contradicted. 'The scouts will be able to masquerade as foreigners and thus avoid speech troubles. The Great Green God could hardly have arranged it better.'

'There are also other impulse streams,' added the technician. 'We suspect them of being pictorial transmissions.'

'Suspect? Don't you *know*?'

'Our receivers cannot handle them, captain.'

'Why not?'

The radio officer said patiently, 'Their methods do not accord with ours. The differences are technical. To explain them would take me a week. In brief, our receivers are not suitable for their transmitted pictures. Eventually, by trial and error methods, we could make them suitable. But it would take a long time.'

'But you do receive their speech?'

'Yes – that is relatively easy.'

'At least, it tells us something. They've got as far as radio. Also, they're vocal and therefore unlikely to be telepathic. I would cross the cosmos for such bait.' Dismissing the radio officer, he went to the airlock, looked into the night-wrapped forest to see how his scouts were doing.

His strange Rigelian life-sense enabled him to detect their quarry almost at a glance, for life burned in the dark like a tiny flame. There was just such a flame high up a nearby tree. He saw it come tumbling down when the paralysing dart from a scout's gun struck home. The flame flickered on landing but did not die out. The hunter picked it up, brought it into the light. It was a tiny animal with prick ears, coarse, reddish fur and a long, bushy tail.

Soon eight scouts struggled in bearing between them a huge, thickly furred form of ferocious aspect. It was big-pawed, big-clawed and had no tail. It stank like molobater blood mixed with aged cheese. Half a dozen other forms were brought in, two of them winged. All were stiffened by darts, had their eyes closed, were incapable of movement. All were taken to the examiners.

One of the experts came to Id-Wan in due course. He was red-smeared and had an acrid smell.

'Nonmalleable. Every one of them.'

'Bhingho!' exclaimed Id-Wan. 'As are the lower forms, so will be the higher.'

'Not necessarily but very probably,' said the expert, dodging the appearance of contradiction.

'We'll see. Had any of these creatures possessed the power of imitative and ultra-rapid reshaping, I should have had to modify my plans. As it is, I can go right ahead.'

The other responded, 'So far as can be judged from these simple types you should have little trouble with their betters.'

'That's what I think,' agreed Id-Wan. 'We must now get ourselves a sample.'

'We'll need more than that. Two at least. A pair of them would enable us to determine the extent to which individuals differ. If the scouts are left to draw upon their own imaginations in creating differences, they may exaggerate sufficiently to betray themselves.'

'All right, we'll get two,' said Id-Wan. 'Call in the chief of the scouts.'

To the chief of the scouts, Id-Wan said, 'All your captures were of unalterable form.'

'Excellent!' The chief was pleased.

'Pfah!' murmured Bi-Nak.

Id-Wan jerked around. 'What was that remark?'

'Pfah, captain,' admitted Bi-Nak, mentally cursing the efficiency of the rubber ear. As mildly as possible, he added, 'I was considering the paradox of rigid superiority and the pfah popped out.'

'If I were telepathic,' answered Id-Wan, deliberately, 'I would know you for the liar you are.'

'Now there's something,' offered Bi-Nak, side-tracking the insult. 'So far we've encountered not one telepathic species. On this planet there are superior forms believed to be rigid – so whence comes their superiority? Perhaps they are telepathic.'

Id-Wan complained to the chief scout, 'Do you hear him? He points and pops out and invents obstacles. Of all the navigators available I had to be burdened with this one.'

'What could be better could also be worse,' put in Po-Duk, for no reason whatsoever.

Id-Wan yelled, 'And this other one hangs around mouthing evasions.' His fur switched from green to blue.

They all went blue, Po-Duk being the slowest. He was almost a colour-cripple, as everyone knew. Id-Wan glared at him, swiftly changed to a reticulated molobater. That caught all three flat out. Id-Wan excelled at molobaters and gained much satirical satisfaction from watching their mutual writhings as each strove to be first. 'See,' he snapped, when finally they had assumed the new shape, 'You are not so good, any of you.'

'No, captain, we are very bad,' endorsed Bi-Nak, oozing the characteristic molobater stench.

Id-Wan eyed him irefully, as if about to criticize the stink, but decided to let the matter drop and turn his attention to the chief of the scouts. He pointed to the photographs. 'There is that encampment a little to our south. As you can see, it is connected by a long, winding path to a narrow road which ambles far over the horizon before it joins a bigger road. The place is fairly isolated; that is why we picked it.'

'Picked it?' echoed the chief.

'We chose it and purposefully landed near it,' Id-Wan explained. 'The lonelier the source of samples, the less likelihood of discovery at the start and the longer before an alarm can be broadcast.'

'Ah!' said the chief, recovering the wits strained by sudden molobating. 'It is the usual technique. We are to raid the camp for specimens?'

'Two of them,' confirmed Id-Wan. 'Any two you can grab without raising premature opposition.'

'That will be easy.'

'It cannot be otherwise. Would we be here, doing what we are doing, if all things did not come easy to our kind?'

'No, captain.'

'Very well. Go get them. Take one of the radio technicians with you. He will first examine the place for signs of a transmitter or any other mode of ultra-rapid communication which cannot be detected on this photograph. If there proves to be some kind of message-channel it must be put out of action, preferably in a manner which would appear accidental.'

'Do we go right now?' asked the chief. 'Or later?'

'At once, while it remains dark. We have observed how their cities dim by night, watched their lights go out, their traffic thin down. Obviously they are not nocturnal. They are most active in the daytime. Get those samples as quickly as possible and be back here before dawn.'

'Right, captain.' The chief went out, still a dutiful molobater but not for long.

Bi-Nak yawned and remarked, 'I am not nocturnal either.'

'You are on duty,' Id-Wan reminded him, severely, 'until I see fit to say that you are not on duty. And furthermore, I am disinclined to declare you off duty so long as I remain at my post.'

'Example is better than precept,' approved Po-Duk, currying favour.

Id-Wan promptly turned on him and bawled, 'Shut up!'

'He was only pointing out,' observed Bi-Nak, picking his not-teeth with fingers that weren't.

Kampenfeldt lumbered with elephantine tread to where three men were lounging full length on the grass. He wiped his forehead as he came but it was from sheer habit. The sun was partway up and beginning to warm. The cool of the morning was still around. Kampenfeldt wasn't sweating, nevertheless he mopped.

One of the reclining men rolled lackadaisically onto one side, welcomed him with 'Always on the run, Ollie. Why don'tcha flop down on the fat and absorb some sun once in while?'

'Never get the chance.' Kampenfeldt mopped again and looked defeated. 'I'm searching for Johnson and Greer. Every morning it's the same — somebody's late for breakfast.'

'Aren't they in their hut?' asked a second man, sitting up with an effort and plucking idly at blades of grass.

'No. First place I looked. Must've got up mighty early because nobody saw them go. Why won't people tell me they're going out and might be late? Am I supposed to save something for them or not?'

'Let 'em do without,' suggested the second man, lying down again and shading his eyes.

'Serves them right,' added the first.

'They're not anywhere around,' complained Kampenfeldt, 'and they didn't go out the gate.'

'Probably climbed the logs,' offered one. 'They've done it before. Most times they climb the logs when they go moonlight fishing. A pair of loonies. Anyone who wanders around like that in the middle of the night has got a hole in his head.' He glanced at his listener. 'Were their rods in the hut?'

'Didn't think to look,' admitted Kampenfeldt.

'Don't bother to look. They've taken them with them, that's a sure bet. They like to show they're tough. Let 'em be tough. It's a free country.'

'Yes,' agreed Kampenfeldt, reluctantly. 'But they ought to have told me about their breakfasts. Now they'll be wasted unless I eat them myself.'

They watched him waddle away, still worried, and mopping his face at regular intervals.

One said, 'That silhouette shows there isn't much wasted.'

Another said, 'Hah!' shaded his eyes with one hand and tried to look at the sun.

An examiner appeared, red-smeared and acrid-smelling as before. 'They're like all the others – fixed in form.'

'Unalterable?' insisted Id-Wan.

'Yes, Captain.' Distastefully he gazed down at the lurid stains upon himself, added, 'Eventually we separated them, putting them in different rooms, and revived them. We killed one, then the other. The first fought with his limbs and made loud noises but displayed no exceptional powers. The other one, in the second room, was already agitated but did not become more so during this time. It was obvious that he had no notion of what was happening to his companion. We then killed him after he had resisted in the same manner. The conclusion is that they are neither hypnotic nor telepathic. They are remarkably ineffectual even at the point of death.'

'Good!' exclaimed Id-Wan, with great satisfaction. 'You have done well.'

'That is not all, captain. We have since subjected the bodies to a thorough search and can find no organs of life-sense. Evidently they have no way of perceiving life other than by ordinary sight.'

'Better still,' enthused Id-Wan. 'No life-sense no dynamic receivers, no way of tuning an individual life and tracing its whereabouts. So those in the camp cannot tell where these two have gone.'

'They couldn't in any case, by this time,' the other pointed out, 'since both are dead.' He tossed a couple of objects onto a table. 'They had these things with them. You may wish to look at them.'

Id-Wan picked up the articles as the examiner went away. They were a pair of small shoulder-bags or satchels made of treated animal hide, well finished, highly polished and attached to adjustable belts.

He tipped their contents out upon the table and pawed through them. A couple of long, flat metal cases containing white tubes stuffed with herbs. Two metal gadgets, similar but not the same, which could be made to spark and produce a flame. A thin card with queer, wriggly writing on one side and a coloured picture of a tall-towered city on the other. One small magnifying glass. Two writing instruments, one black, the other silvery. A crude time-meter with three indicators and a loud tick. Several insect-like objects with small sharp hooks attached. Four carefully folded squares of cloth of unknown purpose.

'Humph!' He scooped the lot back, tossed the satchels to Po-Duk. 'Take them to the workshop, tell them to make six reasonably good copies complete with contents. They must be ready by next nightfall.'

'Six?' queried Po-Duk. 'There will be eight scouts.'

'Imbecile! You are holding the other two.'

'So I am,' said Po-Duk, gazing fascinatedly at the objects as if they had just materialized from thin air.

'There are times and there are times,' remarked Bi-Nak as Po-Duk departed.

Id-Wan let it pass. 'I must have a look at these bodies. I am curious about them' He moved off to the operating rooms, Bi-Nak following.

The kidnapped and slaughtered creatures proved to be not as repulsive as some they'd found on other worlds. They lay side by side, long, lean, brown-skinned, with two arms, two legs, and with dark-coarse hair upon their heads. Their dead eyes were not greatly different from Rigelian eyes. Their flesh was horribly firm despite that it was full of red juice.

'Primitive types,' pronounced Id-Wan, poking at one of them. 'It's a marvel that they've climbed as high as they have.'

'Their digits are surprisingly dexterous,' explained the head examiner. 'And they have well developed brains, more so than I had expected.'

'They will need all their brains,' promised Id-Wan. 'We are too advanced to be served by idiots.'

'That is true,' interjected Bi-Nak, gaining fresh heart.

'Although sometimes I wonder,' added Id-Wan, staring hard at him. He shifted his attention back to the examiner. 'Give these cadavers to the scouts and tell them to get in some practice. I'll pick out the best eight imitators tonight. They had better be good!'

'Yes, captain.'

The sinking sun showed no more than a sliver of glowing rim on a distant hill when the chief of the scouts reported to Id-Wan. There was a coolness creeping over the land but it was not coldness. Here, at this time, the nights were merely less warm than the days.

Id-Wan asked, 'Did you have any difficulty in obtaining those two specimens this morning?'

'No, captain. Our biggest worry was that of getting there before broad daylight. It took longer than we'd anticipated to reach the place. In fact dawn was already showing when we arrived. However, we were lucky.'

'In what way?'

'Those two were already outside the camp, just as if the Great Green God had provided them for us. They bore simple apparatus for trapping water game and evidently intended an early morning expedition. All we had to do was plant darts in them and take them away. They had no chance to utter a sound. The camp slumbered undisturbed.'

'And what about the message channels?'

'The technician could find none,' said the chief. 'No overhead wires, no underground cables, no antenna, nothing.'

'That is peculiar,' remarked Bi-Nak. 'Why should creatures so forward be so backward? They *are* superior types, aren't they?'

'They're relatively unimportant in this world's scheme of things,' declared Id-Wan. 'Doubtless they serve these trees in some way, or watch for fires. It is of little consequence.'

'Sitting down on their dirt is not of little consequence,' grumbled Bi-Nak, strictly to himself. 'I'll be happier after we've blasted one of their towns, or ten of them, or fifty. We can then get their reactions and beat it home with the news. I am more than ready to go home even if I'm chosen to return with the main fleet sometime later.'

'Are the scouts ready for my inspection?' Id-Wan asked the chief.

'Waiting now, captain.'

'All right. I'll look them over.' Going to the rear quarters, he studied the twenty Rigelians lined up against a wall. The two corpses reposed nearby for purposes of comparison. Subjecting each scout to long and careful scrutiny, he chose eight, whereupon the remaining twelve promptly switched to his own shape. The eight were good, very good. Four Johnsons and four Greers.

'It is a simple form to duplicate,' commented the chief. 'I could hold it myself for days on end.'

'Me, too,' agreed Id-Wan. He addressed the row of two-armed, brown-skinned bipeds who could be whatever he wanted them to be. 'Remember the most stringent rule: in no circumstances will you change shape before your task is done. Until then you will retain this precise form and appearance, even under threat of destruction.'

They showed understanding.

He continued, 'All your objectives have large parks into which you will be dropped shortly before dawn. You will then merge as unobtrusively as possible with the creatures appearing in each awakening town. After that, do as you've done many a time before: dig up all the useful data you can get without arousing suspicion. Details of weapons and power sources are especially needed. Enter no building until you are sure that your entry will not be challenged. Do not speak or let yourselves be spoken to if it is avoidable. In the last resort, respond with imitations of a different speech pattern.'

'*Fanziki moula? S finadacta bu!*' said Bi-Nak, helpfully concocting an example.

Id-Wan paused to scowl at him before he went on, 'Above all, be circumspect. Don't let zeal tempt you into betrayal. After all, there are eight of you and any one may find what another has missed.'

They nodded again, humanlike, bipeds all of them but with the Rigelian life-flame burning within them.

He finished, 'If absolutely imperative give up the quest and hide yourselves until the time for return. Be at your respective dropping-points in the parks at the mid-hour of the following night. You will then be picked up.' He raised his voice in emphasis. 'And do not change shape before then.'

They didn't. They had not altered by as much as one hair when they filed impassively into the ship's lifeboat between the mid-hour and the dawn. Id-Wan was there to give them a final look over. Each walked precisely as the now dead samples had walked, swinging his arms in the same manner, using the same bearing and wearing the same facial expression. Each had a satchel complete with alien contents plus a midget dart-gun.

The life-boat rose among the trees, into the dark, bore them away. A few creatures in the trees resented the brief disturbance and made squawking sounds.

'Not one other ship in the night,' remarked Id-Wan, looking upward. 'Not one rocket-trail across the stars. They've got nothing but those clumsy air-machines which we saw toiling through the clouds.' He gave a sigh. 'In due time we'll take over this planet like taking a karda-fruit from a nodus. It is all too easy, too elementary. Sometimes I feel that a little more opposition might be interesting.'

Bi-Nak decided to let that point go for what it was worth, which wasn't a lot in his opinion. Two days and nights on continual duty with the indefatigable Id-Wan had tired him beyond argument. So he yawned, gave the stars a sleepless, disinterested eye and followed Id-Wan into the ship.

Making for the dynamic receivers, Id-Wan had a look at their recording globes each of which had been tuned to a departing scout. Each globe held a bright spot derived from a distant life-glow. He watched the spots shrink with distance until eventually they remained still. A bit later the lifeboat came back and reported all safely landed. The spots continued to shine without shifting. None moved until the sun stabbed a red ray in the east.

Planting another filled glass on the tray, Ollie Kampenfeldt gloomed at a night-shrouded window and said, 'It's been dark two hours. They've been gone all day. No breakfast, no dinner, no supper, nothing. A fellow can't live on nothing. I don't like it.'

'Me neither,' approved somebody. 'Maybe something's happened.'

'If one had broken his leg or his neck, the other would be here to tell us,' another pointed out. 'Besides, if it were anyone else I'd suggest a search for them. But we all know those two yumps. It isn't the first time Johnson and Greer have taken to the jungle. Reckon they've seen too many Tarzan pictures. Just a pair of overgrown muscle-bound kids.'

'Johnson's no kid,' denied the first. 'He's an ex-navy heavyweight who still likes to jump around.'

'Aw, probably they've got lost. It's the easiest thing in the world to get lost if you wander a bit. Four times I've had to camp out all night and – '

'I don't like it,' interjected Kampenfeldt, firmly.

'All right, so you don't like it. What are you going to do about it? Phone the cops?'

'There's no phone, as you well know,' said Kampenfeldt. 'Who'd run a line this far into the wilds?' He thought it over, frowning fatly, and wiped his forehead. 'I'll give 'em to morning. If they're not back by then I'll send Sid on his motorcycle to tell the forest rangers. Nobody's going to say I sat on my butt and did nothing about it.'

'That's the spirit, Ollie,' one of them approved. 'You look after Nature's children and they'll look after you.'

Several laughed at that, heartily. Within half an hour Johnson and Greer were forgotten.

It was early in the afternoon when the tracer operators rushed into the main cabin and so far forgot themselves as not to match Id-Wan's shape. Remaining rotund, tentacular and pale purple, the leading one of the three gesticulated excitedly as he spoke.

'Two have gone, captain.'

'Two what have gone where?' demanded Id-Wan, glowering at him.

'Two dynamic sparks have vanished.'

'Are you certain?' Without waiting for a reply, Id-Wan ran to the receivers.

It was true enough. Six globes still held their tiny lights. Two were dull, devoid of any gleam. Even as he watched another became extinguished. Then, in rapid succession, three more.

The chief of the scouts came in saying, 'What's the matter? Is something wrong?'

Slowly, almost ponderously, Id-Wan replied, 'Six scouts

have surrendered life in the last few moments.' He breathed heavily, seemed to have trouble in accepting the evidence of the globes. 'These instruments say they are dead and if indeed they are dead they cannot retain shape. Their bodies automatically will revert to the form of their fathers. And you know what that means – '

'A complete giveaway,' said the chief of the scouts, staring grimly at the globes.

Both remaining lights went out.

'Action stations!' yelled Id-Wan, electrified by the sight. 'Close all ports! Trim the tubes! Prepare for take-off!' He turned savagely upon Po-Duk. 'You're pilot. Don't squat there like an ebelmint halfway out of its egg. Get into the control-seat, idiot – we've no time to lose!'

Something whisked hell-for-leather overhead. He caught a fleeting glimpse of it through the nearest observation-port. Something long, shapely and glistening but much too fast to examine. It had gone almost before it registered. Its noise followed a long way behind it, a terrible howl.

The radio technician said, 'Powerful signals nearby. Their sources seem to be – '

The ship's tubes coughed, spluttered, spewed fire and coughed again. Outside, a tree began to burn beyond the rim of those already destroyed. Its smoke made a signal visible for miles. Id-Wan danced with impatience. He dashed to the control-room.

'Blast, Po-Duk, blast!'

'There is not yet enough lift, captain, and the meters show that – '

'Look!' screamed Bi-Nak, pointing for the last time.

Through the facing port they could see what was coming: seven ultra-rapid dots in V-formation. The dots lengthened as they neared, and sprouted wings. They shot immediately overhead without a sound. Black lumps poured from their bellies, came down, struck the ship and all around the ship.

The badly lagging noise of the planes never got that far;

their leading waves were repulsed by the awful thunder of the bombs.

For the final change, the Rigelians became a cloud of scattered molecules.

Settling himself more comfortably in the chair, the roving video reporter complained, 'I'd no sooner shown my face in office than the area supervisor grabbed me, told me to rush up here and give the breathless world a candid close-up of mad Martians on the rampage. I'm partway here when the Air Force chips in and holds me back a few hours. When I do get here what do I find?' He sniffed sourly. 'Some timber smoking around a whacking great crater. Nothing else. Not a sausage.'

Dragging an almost endless handkerchief from his pocket, Kampenfeldt smeared it across his brow. 'We keep civilization at arm's length here. We've no telephone, no radio, no video. So I don't know what you're talking about.'

'It's like this,' explained the reporter, 'they dumped their spies in the parks during the night. They weren't around long because they got picked up with the milk. Twenty steps and Clancy had 'em.'

'Eh?'

'The cops,' elucidated the other. 'We put the faces of the first pair on the breakfast-time videocast. Ten viewers phoned in a hurry and identified them as Johnson and Greer. So we assumed that the said Johnson and Greer were off their heads.' He gave a lugubrious laugh.

'Sometimes I've thought so myself,' Kampenfeldt said.

'Then, half an hour later, the next station on the chain infringed our copyright by also showing Johnson and Greer. Another followed suit ten minutes later still. By ten o'clock there were four pairs of them, as alike as two of you, and all grabbed in similar circumstances, exhibiting themselves in public parks. It looked as if the whole cockeyed world wanted to be Johnson or, alternatively, Greer.'

'Not me,' denied Kampenfeldt. 'Neither of them. Not at any price.'

'The news value of that was, of course, way up at the top. The stations collaborated and put the entire eight of them on the mid-morning boost which is nationwide, our only thought being that we'd got hold of something mighty queer. Military intelligence characters in Washington saw the broadcast, pestered local cops for details, put two and two together and made it four, if not eight.'

'And then?'

'They leaned very heavily on all these Johnsons and Greers. They gave 'em what some call, with a light laugh, the treatment. Well, they talked all right but nothing they said made sense. Eventually one of them tried a fast escape and was killed in mid-sprint. He was still Johnson when he went down with a thud but a minute later his body turned into something else, something right out of this world. Gee-whiz, it would have turned your stomach.'

'In that case, I want no description,' informed Kampenfeldt, nursing his paunch.

'That was a real eye-opener. Anything not of this world obviously must be from some other. The authorities became extremely tough with the remaining seven who behaved as before until they realized that we knew what we knew. Forthwith they put death before dishonour, leaving us with eight dollops of goo and no details.'

'Ugh!' said Kempenfeldt.

'Our only clue lay in Johnson and Greer. Since these creatures had copied real people, the thing to do was find the last known whereabouts of said people. Chances were good that alien invaders would be found in that vicinity. A shout went up for the real Johnson and Greer. Umpteen friends of theirs said they were here, right here. Then the forest rangers chipped in saying you'd just reported them missing.'

'I did,' agreed Kampenfeldt. 'And if I'd known where they'd gone I'd be missing myself – and still running.'

'Well, the Air Force took over. They were told to have a look. If an alien ship was down, it was to stay down. You know those boys; they swoop around yipping. They overdid the job and left not a sliver of metal as big as my finger. So what do I put on the videocast? Just a crater and some smoking tree stumps.'

'Which is no great pity,' opined Kampenfeldt. 'Who wants to see things that could climb into your bed pretending to be Uncle Willie? You wouldn't know who was who with creatures like that around.'

'You would not.' The reporter brooded awhile, added, 'Their simulation was perfect. They had the power to lead us right up the garden path if only they'd known how to use it. Power is never much good unless you know how to use it. They made a first-class blunder when they grabbed their models.' He scratched his head, eyed the other speculatively. 'It sure beats me that of all places in this wide world they had to pick on a nudist camp.'

'Solar health centre,' corrected Kampenfeldt, primly.

ULTIMA THULE

The rocket-ship came shivering out of hyperspace and solidified. Metallic coldness slid over its surface, starting from the prow, spreading to the tail. The pale ghosts of forty main propulsors were the last to gain concrete form. They hardened, became a quadruple ring of tubes ready to blast eight miles of fire.

Lawder, peering through the bow observation port, wiped his eyes. He had been there much longer than usual, much longer. A nervous hand reached for binoculars. The high-powered glasses could not have been of much use, the way they shook. He put them down, wiped the eyes again.

'What's eating you?' Santel was watching him. 'Is something wrong?'

'Plenty.'

It brought Santel upright, running long fingers through red hair. He stalked to the port, stared through.

'Well?' invited Lawder.

'Impossible!'

'Ha!' Lawder said.

Santel tried the binoculars, resting wrists on the port's thick rim to steady the field of vision.

'Well?' Lawder persisted.

'Impossible,' maintained Santel.

'You deny the evidence of your own eyes?'

'First impressions can be misleading.'

'We're lost.' Lawder sat down, viewed his boots without seeing them. His thin face twitched. 'Lost souls in a pitch black hell.'

'Shut up!'

'When I was a kid I once put three flies in a bottle. Then I rammed home the cork. That's us, flies in a bottle.'

'Shut up!' repeated Santel more loudly. His red hair was stiff, bristly. He had another look through the port. 'I'm telling Vanderveen.'

'I threw the bottle into a lake. That was thirty years ago, several fly-lifetimes ago. In a lake, cold and dark, without a shore. They're still there maybe. Still there maybe. Still there, corked in.'

Switching the intercom, Santel spoke into its mike. His voice was hoarse.

'Captain, there's something odd. Better come along and see.'

'I can see from here,' boomed the loudspeaker.

'Huh?'

'There are four windows in this navigation room. They are there to be looked through. I have looked.'

'What d'you make of it?'

'Nothing.'

'Lost,' murmured Lawder. 'Become as if we had never been. Another lonely line on the list of missing ships. Memories that thin with the years and eventually drift away.'

'One can only make nothing of nothing,' said Captain Vanderveen. 'Who's that mumbling in there?'

'Lawder.'

'Who else could it be?' shouted Lawder at the loud-speaker. 'There are only we three. All together and all alone. Just three of us. You and me and Santel.'

'How can three be alone?' asked Vanderveen gently. 'Only one man can be alone, or one woman, one child.'

'Woman – we'll never see one.' Lawder's knuckles were white. 'Children – we'll never know one.'

'Take it easy,' advised Santel, looking at him.

'There's a quart of Tralian alodine in the second drawer,' came Vanderveen's voice. 'Give him a double shot. I'll be along in a minute.'

Lawder gulped it down, breathed heavily. After a while he said, 'Sorry, Santel.'

'It's all right.'

'Sort of shook me up a bit.'

'I know.'

'You don't know.' He showed the signet ring on his left hand. 'She gave me this two months ago. I gave her pinfire opals from Procyon Seven. We were to be married soon. This was to be my last trip.'

'So!' Santel's eyebrows lifted slightly.

'It will be my last all right.'

'Now, now,' soothed Santel.

'My last, forever. She can wait, watching the calendar, haunting the spaceports, scanning the arrival lists, hoping, praying. She can grow old and grey without news. Or find someone else. Someone who'll come back to her, laughing, with gifts.' His hand went out. 'Give me that bottle again.' He gurgled lengthily, held it up, studied its dark glass. 'Flies, that's us.'

'Your childhood conscience is biting back at you,' Santel diagnosed. 'You shouldn't have done it.'

'Didn't you ever cork them in?'

'No.'

'Or pull off their wings and watch them crawl?'

'No.'

'You're lucky.'

'So it seems.' Dryly, Santel nodded towards the port.

Vanderveen lumbered in, a huge man, portly, with a great spade-beard.

'So you have gazed through the windows and do not like

it.' He was probably the only experienced deep-spacer who persisted in referring to observation ports as windows. 'You look only through these and not through the others. How silly.'

They reacted eagerly. 'You have seen something, Captain?'

'Nothing. Through every window it is the same. There is nothing.'

They relaxed, disappointed.

'There is now only one unobserved direction,' he went on. 'That is tailward. One of you had better put on a spacesuit. No need to go through the bow lock. The main drivers are cold and will give direct rearward view.'

Santel dressed himself. They tightened the neck-bolts of his helmet. He went out.

Every sound of his motion could be heard throughout the ship, faithfully conducted, a little amplified. The clump of his boots. The clang of the engine room's airtight doors. A thin, shrill whistle of air being pumped away before he opened the inspection-trap of a vacuum-filled combustion chamber. Slithering noises outward then inward. All the former sounds in reverse order.

He returned. They knew the answer before they unwound the neck-bolts. It was depicted on his face behind the plastiglass visor. The helmet came off. A dampness lay over his forehead.

'It's a heck of a lot worse when you look straight out at it.' Santel split his suit down the front, wriggled like a crab escaping its shrunken shell. 'And it's wrong, terribly wrong.'

'Blackness,' chattered Lawder, flourishing his bottle. 'Sheer, solid, unrelieved blackness. Not a spark. Not one gold or silver gleam. Not a pale pink rocket trail. Not a phantom comet.'

Vanderveen stood by a port, pawing his beard.

'No suns, no planets, no green fields, no singing birds,'

Lawder went on. He poured generously down his gullet. 'The Lord hath given and the Lord hath taken away.'

'He's getting drunk,' warned Santel.

'Let him.' Vanderveen did not look around. 'He to his inward comforts – we to ours.'

Santel said steadily, 'Maybe I'm slower on the uptake. I don't yet feel ready for despair.'

'Of course not. You're an engineer and therefore have an engineer's mind. You know we can try the hyperdrive and chance where it takes us. Or the rockets. We have vanished from the ken of men but we're not yet beaten.'

'Yes, the hyperdrive.' It hit home in Lawder's brain. 'Twenty light-years in one hour. That will save us. What gets in can always come out.' He grinned around, momentarily happy.

'Like an aeroplane plunging into the sea,' suggested Santel. 'Gets in. Doesn't like it. Up she goes.'

Lawder swayed close to him, the bottle a glass bludgeon in his grip, swinging it hot-handed.

'You don't care if we rot here for ever. What have *you* got to go back to? One lousy room in a stinking hostel for lousy spacemen. A month aground picking your teeth and snoring through a library of slumber-educators for the big-ship rating you'll never get. Living and longing for the spaceways that will land you no place when your day is done and – '

'That will do, Lawder,' snapped Vanderveen.

'As for you – ' Lawder turned to him.

'THAT WILL DO!' Vanderveen's beard stuck out. His big hands were bunched.

Savagely, Lawder swung the bottle, sobbing, 'Talk to me like that!'

The captain grunted deep down in his chest, thrust out a huge paw. No more. He did no more than that but it sent the other headlong across the room.

Silence. They stared at the body slumped in a corner, eyes shut, breathing slowly and without sound. Turning, they looked through the port. Silence. Blackness. No far-away lanterns. No faint aureate glow of a Milky Way. Only the utter deadliness of the day before Creation. They were bodies on a forgotten barge becalmed in an ageless, endless sea. A sable sea dark and peaceful, as death.

'Spacemen don't get that way.' Santel jerked a thumb toward the corner. 'He can't be normal.'

'He has someone waiting. That means much.'

Santel cocked an eye at him. 'What of you?'

'I am not soon to be married.' The captain viewed the dark, seeing only the past. 'Besides, I am different. You are different. That is our beauty as men, that all are different. Each does his best with what the good Lord has given him. He can do no more.'

'No, sir,' agreed Santel, very respectfully.

Lawder came round after a bit, blinked blearily, made no remark. Crawling into his bunk, he snored for four hours. He awoke, had a look at the chronometer.

'You fellows been standing there all that time?'

'Most of it.'

'Gaping at jet-black nothingness? What good will it do you?'

Santel did not bother to answer.

'We've been thinking,' said Vanderveen 'Hard.'

'Yeah?' Lawder crawled out of his bunk, stood up, tenderly felt around his chops. 'Who socked me?'

'Maybe I did. Or maybe Santel did. Or maybe you conked yourself with that bottle you were waving around.'

'I get it. Nobody's telling.'

'So long as I'm captain there are going to be no recriminations, no animosities. Not while we're in this fix. We're too small a bunch, too dependent upon each other.'

Lawder eyed him, licked dry lips. 'I guess you're right. Well, I'll go get a drink. I feel dehydrated.'

'Easy on the water,' advised Vanderveen.

'Eh?'

'There's only so much.'

Easy on the water – there's only so much. That was today, the first day. Tomorrow, next week, next month – what? Rationing by count of drops, every one more precious than its predecessor. Each man's measure watched avidly by other eyes, lingering on every glistening globule, seeing it stretch, drop, and hearing its sweet, delicious *plop!*

And three minds growing increasingly bemused by the simple mathematics of the situation: a two-way split goes farther than a three-way deal. Higher calculus: all for one is more than for two. How much consumable blood in somebody else's body? Would the biggest one hold the most? How many warm pints in Vanderveen?

The captain's gaze was on him as he went for his drink. It would have been easier to bear had it been accusing, suspicious or threatening. But it was not. It was cool, calm, courageous. That made it hard, so hard. Lawder contented himself with a mere suck rolled around his mouth. He came slowly back.

'Are we to squat here until we're mummified? Why don't we take to hyperdrive again?'

Vanderveen's thick finger pointed outside. 'Because we don't know which way to shoot. Direction is a path relative to visible things. There is nothing visible, therefore there are no means of relating ourselves to anything, no sense of direction.'

'We know how we're sitting. All we need to do is back out along the line we came in.'

'I wish it were that easy.' If the captain was worried he did not show it. 'We don't know how we're sitting or even whether we are sitting at all. We may be motionless or not. We may have rotated a hundred times, longitudinally, or axially, and remained unaware of it. We may be skidding some place in a straight line, at high velocity, or we may be curving around an enormous arc. There's just no way of telling.'

'But the instruments – '

'The instruments were designed for the space-time continuum in which they were made. Right now we need *new* instruments for a totally different set of circumstances.'

'All right. I'll give you that. But we've still got the hyperdrive.' Lawder gestured urgently. 'It can jerk us through four successive layers of hyperspace, four co-existing universes. They won't all be blotted out like this hell-hole. They'll have lights, beacons, calling us home.'

'Beacons,' echoed Santel moodily. 'One red dwarf, old and sterile and planetless, would look like heaven to me.'

'We can try, can't we?' insisted Lawder. 'Can't we?'

'We can.' Vanderveen was thoughtful, reluctant. 'But if we choose wrongly – '

'We'll be another mighty jump still deeper into the dark,' Santel finished for him. 'Then we'll go nuts and make another and another. Getting farther and farther away while trying to get nearer. Struggling harder and sinking deeper like flies trapped in sticky beer.'

'Flies!' Lawder shouted at the top of his voice. 'You throw those up at me? Why, you – !'

Vanderveen moved forward, almost touching him chest to chest. 'Be quiet! Listen!' His fingers combed a moment at his great beard. 'We have a multitude of choices. Port, starboard, ahead, astern, upward, downward and thousands of intermediates. Plus all the other co-ordinates which make the number of chances a string of figures ten yards long. Only one of those may be correct. Only one may give us salvation, life, home, the green fields, the friendly sun, the warmth and fellowship of other men. Any of the others may make confusion worse confounded, our damnation more damned. Do you understand that?'

'Yes.' It came out in a whisper.

'Very well. Give me a direction and we'll try it.'

'Me?' Lawder was shaken. 'Why me?'

'You're the bellyacher,' said Santel.

The captain turned on him. 'That was unnecessary.' Again to Lawder. 'Go on, choose!'

'How?' Lawder stalled for time, fearful of error.

'Point.' Vanderveen's lips uttered it again, commandingly. '*Point!*'

Perspiring freely, Lawder stuck out an arm at random. It was like giving the signal for the death-trap to be sprung.

'Give me a three-figure number,' Vanderveen ordered.

'237.'

'A letter.'

'B.'

'And an angle.'

'Forty-seven degrees.'

To Santel. 'You heard what he said. Set them up along the line he picked. Switch immediately you're ready.'

Ceremoniously, Santel dragged a tiny woollen monkey from his breast pocket, patted it three times, kissed it once, stuffed it back. He sat at the control board, adjusted it and switched.

The others stood waiting as if it were normal for the hyperdrive to be subject to delay. It was merely that its unexpected lack of response took a little while to sink into their minds. Not a shudder, not a shake. No queer, flesh-tingling twist such as always accompanied ultra-rapid transition from one scheme of things to another. Not even the faintest tremor in the fabric of the ship.

Scowling to himself, Santel set the controls anew, tried again, reset, had a third go. He disappeared into the engine room, came back after twenty minutes, tried the controls.

'It won't work.' His face came round over one shoulder, showing features strained and mystified. 'There is nothing wrong with the apparatus. Everything is as it ought to be. Yet it doesn't function.'

Lawder burst out, 'It has *got* to.'

'In that case,' suggested Santel, leaving the board, 'you make it work.'

'I'm not the engineer. That's your job.'

'Well, I've flopped on it. I can't put right something that isn't wrong. I can't cure mechanical or electronic faults that don't exist. See if you can do better.'

'Let me try.' Vanderveen pushed past, sat at the board, patiently set up a dozen series of co-ordinates. He switched each one in turn. The vessel did not stir. Its ports remained blank and jet-black as if immersed in soot. 'No luck.' He arose heavily, without visible emotion, but somehow aged and tired. 'The drive is out for keeps.'

Santel ran fingers through his hair and said, 'I don't like this, captain. Hyperdrive operates from space to space. In theory there is only one place where it cannot work.'

'Well?'

'Unspace or not-space or whatever you care to call it. Somewhere completely devoid of spatial properties.'

'Bunk?' Lawder chipped in emphatically. 'Everywhere has got to be within one continuum or another. Where could not-space be?'

Vanderveen said, 'Outside the whole of Creation.'

Momentarily it hypnotized both of them. They stood there, side by side, viewing him with dazed eyes, their thoughts stirred to turmoil, their tongues locked and growing dry.

Finally, Lawder found voice. 'The big boats can go faster and farther than us. They can cross gulfs between island universes, hyperspatially. They've skipped from one galaxy to another and found more beyond. Always there are more beyond, an endless procession of them sparkling in the dark. Creation has no limits.'

'Hasn't it?'

'No,' declared Lawder, flatly.

'Can you *think* of it without limits?'

'The human mind can't really conceive infinity. So what?'

'So you're dogmatically asserting that which you cannot

conceive.' Vanderveen studied him beneath thick brows. 'Not that that proves or disproves anything.'

'Do some proving of your own,' Lawder invited. He was getting excited as his mind absorbed the dreadful implications of the captain's viewpoint.

Vanderveen said quietly, 'The hyperdrive is extremely efficient when it works but it's not one hundred per-cent reliable. It operates in and through any space continuum. Here it does not work. Neither is light transmitted any-where immediately outside the ship. Neither does the radio respond.'

'The radio.' Lawder smacked his forehead in self-reproof. 'I forgot it.'

'We tried it while you were snoring. It remains as silent as the grave.' Clasping hands behind him, the captain paced the room. 'We are some place that is not space as we understand it. Somewhere cold and sterile. Somewhere devoid of all gravitational and electromagnetic phenomena. That which stands outside of all material things and all creative forces. Negativity. Ultima Thule. The place that God forgot.' He stared at them, his beard protruding. 'The hyperdrive hit a rut and we got tossed right out of mundane existence.'

'That's how it's beginning to look to me,' Santel admitted. 'All the things with which we are familiar – light, gravitation, air, food, warmth, company and so on – are confined within this vessel. Outside is nothing – except, possibly, faraway and buried deep in the dark, the forty-odd ships which have vanished without a word or trace in the three thousand years since hyperdrive came into general use. Gone forever,' droned Santel, seeming to find morbid pleasure in it. 'Forever and forever, amen!'

Lawder declaimed furiously, 'We'll show up. We'll come zooming back in a blaze of glory. We won't stay stuck until kingdom come. Do you know why?' He glowered at one, then the other, inviting contradiction. 'Because I'm going to start the rockets.'

'Useless,' Santel told him. 'One hour of hyperdrive covers more distance than the rockets could make in twenty years, even if the fuel – '

'Damn the fuel! May you both burn with it!'

They were silent. Their gaze followed him as he took the pilot's seat, operated the injectors, pressed the firing-stud. The ship roared and shuddered.

'See?' He came out of the seat, yelled above the noise, did a little dance of triumph. 'See?'

'See?' shouted Santel even louder. He pointed to the meters. Their needles quivered in sympathy with the vessel's trembling, but that was all. No forward thrust. No velocity. No acceleration rate. Only the thermometer responded. It began to climb rapidly. Warmth poured inward from the tail-end, there being almost no radiation outward.

'Cut it out, Lawder,' commanded Vanderveen, anxiously noting the rise of the red line. 'Cut it out – or we'll be roasted alive.'

'Roast,' howled Lawder, ignoring the meters and doing a crazy jig. 'Who cares? We're going back. Home. Among the trees and flowers. Winifred there, smiling, happy.' The rockets bellowed. Heat built up. Sweat began to run down his cheeks and was not noticed in his exultation. 'Winifred, for me. Home. We're on the way.'

'Space-happy,' commented Santel, grim.

'Lawder, I said cut it out.'

'Back to the suns, the moons, the seas, the clouds. Back to people, millions of them. Thanks to me. The bottle is uncorked, thanks to me.'

'CUT IT OUT!' Vanderveen lumbered forward, hair lank, beard dripping. The red line was three-quarters up.

'Never! Never! We're going back, I tell you. Whether you like it or not.' His eyes went cunning as they watched the captain's approach. 'Keep away. The rockets will run without your orders. Keep away!' pulling open the pilot's drawer, he made a grab inside, got something heavy and metallic blue.

A thin stab of fire came from Vanderveen's hip.

Lawder posed by the drawer, one hand propped upon it. He gazed at Vanderveen, his face wet, his eyes softening. The rockets thumbed and thundered. He went slowly to his knees, pulling the drawer out and spilling its contents. Leaping behind him, Santel stopped the flow to the main propulsors.

In the deep silence that followed, Lawder said apologetically, 'I only want home . . . Winifred. You understand?' His voice was like a child's. He shook his head blindly, keeled over, ceased to breathe.

'Last trip.' Santel stood over him, looking down. 'It was his last trip.'

Vanderveen mopped his forehead. 'I intended to make a near miss and frighten him. It was a bad shot.'

'It was fate.'

'A bad shot,' persisted Vanderveen. 'I had little time to think or aim.' He turned away sadly. 'The pain was his but the punishment is mine. I have slaughtered part of myself.'

Santel watched him go out, slow-footed.

No man is an island.

Five weeks. Eight forty Earth hours. Twenty inter-galactic time-units. Aeons in a berillisteel bottle. And still the impenetrable dark outside, thick, cloying, the dark that had never known light or life.

Santel mooched into the navigation room, flopped into a seat. He was thin, pale, had the gauntness of one cooped up with trouble too long.

'The food is all right. Enough for a year. What's the use of it without a year's oxygen?'

Busily writing at his desk, Vanderveen did not reply.

'If we had been fixed up with half an acre of oxygen-producing Sirian cacti, like the big boats carry, we'd have been okay in that respect. Tending them would give us something to do. We could concentrate our worrying upon the water.'

Scribble, scribble, continued Vanderveen.

'Reckon the water will last us about three more weeks unless we reduce our takings still further.'

No response.

'After that – curtains!' He mooned irritably at the captain's broad back. 'Well, aren't you interested?'

Vanderveen sighed, put down his pen, swung round in his seat. 'We share and share alike, to the end.'

'That's understood,' agreed Santel.

'It is not understood.' The other's eyes were sharp and penetrating as they looked into his. 'You have cheated. You have tried to deceive me. For the last ten days you have taken less than your fair share. I know, for I have checked up on it. He paused, added, 'So I have taken similarly less. That makes us quits.'

Flushing, Santel said, 'There was no sense in doing that.'

'Why not?'

'You are twice my size. You need more.'

'What, more life?' He waited for the reply that did not come. 'I am older than you. I have had more life.'

Santel changed the subject with the alacrity of the out-argued. 'Writing, writing, always writing. Is it necessary?'

'I am entering the log in full detail.'

'It won't be read for a million years, if ever. We have departed the mortal coil. We're dead but not quite ready to lie down – though it won't be long now. That makes log-filling a waste of effort, doesn't it?'

'It is my duty.'

'Duty?' Santel gave a sniff of disdain. 'Did Lawder think of duty?'

'In a way.' The captain mused a moment. 'He had an all-absorbing ambition, natural, harmless, involving a woman and an Earthbound home. He had worked hard for it over many years, been denied it over many years, but at last found it almost within reach. In the crisis he did his duty to his dreams, but because his dreams were not ours we thought him a little crazy.' He gestured toward the log. 'So I have written that he died in the line of duty. It is all that I can do for him.'

'And it's a waste of effort,' maintained Santel.

'For five weeks you have been trying various combinations on the hyperdrive. Isn't that equally a waste of effort?'

'One must do something or go nuts. Besides, it is better to live in hope than die in despair.'

'Precisely!' Vanderveen twisted back to his desk and resumed writing, his pen going *scratch-scratch*. 'So I accept to the very last my responsibilities as ship commander. And remote though the chance may be, a full and complete account of what has occurred may be useful to somebody someday. If it served to save the skin of only one ignorant savage it would not be in vain.'

Log-filling. It may be useful someday, somewhere, somehow. The drear, dull grind of routine when life has dribbled away to a mere three weeks, perhaps less. The multi-million to one hope of providing salvation for some barbarian a thousand generations unborn. An impossible long-shot aimed to help one ship or one sailor at a far-distant time when hyperdrives might be hopelessly antiquated and all the multitudinous existences accurately measured, weighed, estimated.

'The least one can do,' added Vanderveen, by way of afterthought, 'is one's duty to the last – as one deems it.'

Santel stood up, staring over the captain's shoulder, seeing the rim of beard that jutted from the stubborn chin. *Scratch-scratch* went the pen. It was like the scratchings of man-hordes at the foundations of Creation. Striving and scratching to bare the treasures and secrets hidden therein; dying and scratching and never giving up.

And it was like the scratching of his dry tongue upon his

dry palate. Water, water. Three weeks. Twice three are six. Three threes are nine. Mistress Mary, quite contrary, how does your garden grow? Water, it needs water. Three weeks. Twice three are six.

'So I have taken similarly less. That makes us quits.'

Quietly Santel went out, closing the door. His gait was stiff, robotlike, his features set. His eyes were on something faraway and insignificant. His dream, his own dream. A scrap of paper. An unimportant roll of vellum bearing the great transcosmic seal above his own name. Engineer First Class. Perhaps the name would have been written with a scratchy pen. All this for that. His dream. How futile.

A little later a thin whistle of air sounded from the front. It rose and fell, sobbing without loudness, in imitation of one who weeps muffled and alone.

Vanderveen heard the last wail of it, dropped his pen. Puzzled, apprehensive, he went to the door, pulled it open.

'Santel!'

Silence.

'Are you there?'

An awful hush.

'SANTEL!'

He raced to the bow, steel-shod boots clattering, his beard jutting forward, his eyes anxious.

There it was, the forward airlock, fastened on the inside, open on the outside, open to the eternal dark. He looked around, big hands clasping and unclasping. Three space-suits hanging nearby, bulgy but slack, like iron men drained of their insides. A note stuck to the middle one.

'I have nobody. You have many. Goodbye.'

Taking it down, he carried it back to the navigation room, sat a long, long, time fingering the note and gazing blankly at the wall. Finally, he picked up his pen.

Another six and a half weeks. Twenty-six inter-galactic time-units.

Vanderveen wrote slowly, laboriously, with screwed up eyes and many pauses for breath. He was not engaged upon the log. That official tome lay to one side, discarded, finished with the day's entry. In that respect, duty was done, to the last. But he was still writing.

The calendar hung upon the wall, its various sector indicators long out of date. The chronometer had stopped. A dozen oxygen inlets were wide open and empty, not a whiff of life coming through their tubes from the depleted tanks at back. The utter blackness of non-existence still lay over the ports, ready for invasion and further conquest when the ship's dimming lights at last flickered and went out.

With strenuous effort he inscribed, 'I am not alone so long as I can see your face within my mind. I am not alone while I have memories of you. I thank you, dearest, for these things you have given me, because of which I am not alone.' He paused to assert his will over his failing hand. 'But now I must finish with fondest love to you and the children, from their affectionate father Conrad V – '

He struggled hard to complete the name, and failed.

The dark came in.

The multitudinous years, the long-rolling aeons cannot be measured in death. There is no time beyond the pale of living things.

So there was no sense of bygone millennia when Vanderveen awoke. There was only brilliant light and much pain and many glistening things in which coloured fluids trembled and bubbled. Also, there were voices deep inside his mind.

'We can do no more. It's now or never. Flip that switch and let's see if he keeps going.'

Pain was all over, along every nerve and artery, in every muscle, but gradually subsiding. The soundless voices were becoming strong.

Something nearby gave a loud click. A torturing throb

within him ceased. Only the slight pulsation of his heart could be felt. He was weak, befuddled and curiously tired.

'VANDERVEEN!' It struck commandingly into the depths of his brain, forcing him to open his eyes and thrust away his lassitude.

He was lying flat on a surface soft, warm and resilient. Three men stood by his side. He knew instinctively that they were men though unlike any he had ever known. None had possessed such huge optics or exuded such mental power.

'You can sense what we are saying?'

A whisper. 'Yes.'

'Beyond the Rim nothing changes, nothing deteriorates. That has saved you.'

'Saved?' He strove to comprehend.

'You have been resuscitated.'

Questions formed haltingly in his mind. Where am I? Who are these? How did I get here?'

They must have been able to read his thoughts, for they responded, 'There can be no deliberate escape from non-space. But Creation expands into it at tremendous rate. Eventually its limits reached your vessel – and life reclaimed its own.'

That was far too much for him to absorb at such a moment. He made no attempt to grapple with the concept, but listened as they went on.

'So ships come back now and again, aeons apart, like relics from the dawn of history. Yours proved to be a treasure of value beyond compute for it contained essential data which will enable us to prevent further disappearances. There will be no more lost vessels, no more, no more.'

It did not gratify him. There were other fears that prevented him from linking up yesterday's duty with today's reward.

'My wife,' he got out in an agony of apprehension.

They shook sad heads, went silent.

He struggled to sit up. 'My children.'

One patted his hand and smiled at him. 'We are your children.'

Of course, they must be. He sank back, closed his eyes. He who serves mankind is part of mankind – and mankind's children are his very own.

A watcher turned a huge scanner, swung it nearer, showed a waiting and hopeful world that the man from seventeen thousand years ago lived once again.

And as it concentrated upon him, Captain Vanderveen slept knowing that he was not alone.